MURDER FOR TREASURE

Could the takeover of Rigley's Patent Footbalm by the
giant American Hutstacker Chemical Corporation
really be scuppered by Mrs Ogmore Davies' parrot
finding a body in Panty Harbour? It looked like it, but
banker sleuth Mark Treasure took a different view
when a second body was discovered the morning after
he arrived in the little West Wales sailing village . . .

MURDER FOR TREASURE

David Williams

·BLACK·
·DAGGER·
·CRIME·

First published 1980
by
William Collins

This edition 2000 by Chivers Press
published by arrangement with
the author

ISBN 0 7540 8559 7

British Library Cataloguing in Publication Data available

Printed and bound in Great Britain by
Redwood Books, Trowbridge, Wiltshire

This one for Elizabeth

CHAPTER 1

Mrs Ogmore-Davies had not been looking for a dead body. What she said later about a premonition was regarded by many as embellishment, but not by older Panty residents who respected Mrs Ogmore-Davies's much advertised psychic powers.

There were others who remained undecided about the whole business. If she had known there was going to be a body in the harbour, why had she not said so to Dai Rees, instead of telling him her parrot Gomer had been blown away again and she was going to fetch him from the harbour to save his having to walk home. That was understandable, especially with the Easter holidays on and the children about: it was well known that Gomer bit children.

If Mrs Ogmore-Davies had said to Dai Rees, 'Dai, there's a body by the water', it stood to reason he would have stopped delivering post and gone with her; in any case, it was mostly circulars he had in his bag—nothing that couldn't have waited. But Dai had been definite: it was only the parrot she had mentioned—that and the wind and the time of day. Even the village elders had to accept as much. They trusted Dai. His grandfather had been a deacon in the days when there had been chapel deacons—and a chapel.

Mind you, Mrs Ogmore-Davies did not state categorically she had told Dai that supernatural forces were impelling her towards the harbour. She only thought she might have implied—through her manner, even—that there was more than Gomer at stake. So there were no other witnesses and you could hardly blame Police Constable Lewin for taking the whole thing with a pinch of salt—psychic powers and all. As it happens, Constable Lewin was wrong, at least about the existence of a body.

It was six-thirty in the morning when Mrs Ogmore-Davies pulled on her late husband's oilskin coat and set off from Mariner's Rest in the direction of the harbour. Her cottage, at the old and top end of Panty High Street, is perched two hundred feet above sea level. Although it had offered the once retired and now deceased Captain Ogmore-Davies a nostalgically commanding view of St Brides Bay, as well as a good deal of the surrounding West Wales coastline, it had been the steep climb back on the next to shortest route from the Boatman Inn, executed twice daily, that had finally precipitated enduring rest for that particular merchant mariner, ten minutes after closing time on a wet night in the previous November.

Tragic as it had been for Mrs Ogmore-Davies to be deprived of her soul-mate through the intervention of fate and the demon drink—officially he had succumbed to heart failure while falling down some area steps—it was not long before she had re-established communication with the departed over what she referred to as the ether. She was thus able to make up for years of frustration and confer with him during opening hours, and if his reported responses were to be credited, then she permitted him a much larger role in the conversation than he had ever enjoyed during nearly half a century of marriage.

Mrs Ogmore-Davies chose the longest route to the harbour, following the descending High Street to sea-level at the head of the cove. She then had to walk back along the recently cobbled track skirting the river estuary to the land-locked and half-tidal harbour directly below her own property. The cobbles—or popple-stones, to use the local name—were as uncomfortable underfoot as some had predicted, but there was a grudging consensus that they added colour and credibility.

In the words of Edwin Egor, Estate Agent and Chartered Surveyor, 'the village of Panty sits astride the coast road 'twixt Haverfordwest and the ancient cathedral seat of St David's'. Until very recent times, it has not so much been long forgotten as never remarked at all. Historically, economically and strategically, it lacked any firm reason for being. Its shallow harbour, approached from seawards via a cliff-hung, twisting inlet, had lent itself to clandestine enterprise such as the export of stolen cows in the sixteenth century and the import of illegal Irish immigrants in the nineteenth, but nothing had happened in between or after.

When the shipment of lead and later iron ore offered other ports in the area periods of reasonable prosperity, Panty had been tried and found too shallow. It had been too far west to profit when coal became the staple export of Wales. Even the lifeboat station established in 1860 had been abandoned two years later, when it was admitted there were too few fishermen in the area to muster an adequate crew.

The emergence and advertisement of Panty as a picturesque old fishing village in the latter part of the twentieth century thus owed more to the property speculators than to historical fact: hence the popple-stones.

The transformation had begun the day after The Mistake. A Panty ploughman, living in an officially condemned and near-derelict dwelling, had been in the act of moving his family and chattels to a new Council house in St David's, when a passing and opportunist tourist from London had made him an offer for the property. The ploughman, a simple and honest fellow, was also a man of few words — and most of those were Welsh. Having shaken hands on what he had understood to be three hundred pounds — a sum in excess of the compensation due to him from the Local Authority — he was so overcome with his good fortune on receiving a cheque for three thousand that he revealed all to the local butcher, who normally obliged with the processing of cheques for those of his customers without bank accounts.

Pausing only to advise the ploughman to keep the whole affair secret, the butcher had closed his shop and promptly applied himself to the ready cash acquisition of other condemned properties in the village, as well as a few that were not. It was only a matter of weeks before the whole story was out, but they were profitable ones for the butcher.

What came to be known as The Mistake was soon established as part of local legend, and the expectancy of all Panty property owners increased forthwith not ten but twentyfold—a tribute to the enduring quality of Welsh optimism despite centuries of disappointment.

At the time of The Mistake, a decade ago, Panty had comprised a cluster of dwellings, most of them high above the harbour, and, as Edwin Egor was to put it, 'atop the proud and rugged coastline', and exposed to the prevailing north wind which blew off the land with such ferocity that even the local oaks grew to resemble inverted giant umbrellas snagged in the act of hurtling seawards.

The few other occupied houses were arranged, Italian style, on irregular terraces between the High Street and the harbour and served by a minor labyrinth of lanes, paths and steps. For the most part, though, the cliff-top heart of Panty had been oriented to connect with the fertile land behind the village, the local breadwinners being mostly employed in agrarian rather than maritime pursuits. The Mistake had changed all that.

Within a year of the famous error 'old fishermen's cottages' were being erected on a wholesale basis. White-washed, pink-washed and unwashed stucco dwellings in 'traditional style' sprang up by the dozen, offering maximum untraditional comforts at matching prices to the foreign—meaning English—weekend sailors queuing to buy them. The harbour acquired a marina complete with a prefabricated wooden yacht club. Disused shops re-opened as boutiques, ships chandlers and outlets for the sale of antique and 'antiqued' brassware. There was a brisk trade in fish netting for adorning walls and patios—plain for indoors and tarred when there was any risk of it getting wet.

Although the buildings in Old Panty had been the first to change hands, and suffer the modernizing process, their numbers were limited and, while they provided a degree of authenticity, they were hardly convenient for those newcomers whose interests centred on the marina and the moorings off shore. Thus it was that New Panty was created—a fresh and alien community clustered around the river estuary close to the bridge at the bottom of the High Street with the broad popple-stoned link to the pleasures of the sea.

It would be an overstatement to say that all who survived (inevitably to be dubbed as Old Panties) were hill dwellers, while all New Panties languished in the river valley, but the division roughly worked that way. Old Panties were, in any case, very much a minority. They consisted in the main of freeholders whose optimism had been so divorced from reality that two property booms had come and gone leaving them and their asking prices still *in situ*, together with those tradespeople who had eschewed short-term gains in favour of the rich rewards offered from the long-term exploitation of the affluent new arrivals.

There remained the Old Panty carriage trade—the doctor, the vicar, and a handful of gentlefolk, who had enjoyed a quiet and fulfilling existence in Panty since before The Mistake. Although they were not exploitable, they were not themselves exploiting. They deserved honouring on both counts.

Numbered among these last was the Judge, who had

long since retired from administering justice in the Colonies—and rather earlier than expected at the time, due more to the increasing eccentricity of his judicial pronouncements than to the decreasing size of the British Empire.

What the original inhabitants lacked in numbers, they made up in homogeneity. The newcomers at best had a hobby in common plus a shared and growing distaste for being fleeced by the locals—loosely binding influences not exactly scenting of the stuff that built nations. In contrast, Old Panties were held together by an influence older than Cadwaladr. They were Welsh, a fact that transcended all other considerations—allowing for a modicum of licence where large sums of money might be involved.

'Go-mer! Go-mer!' Mrs Ogmore-Davies's powerful mezzo-soprano summons carried seawards and echoed against the cliffs as she progressed along the quayside in the half-light and the morning drizzle, her substantial figure swaddled from neck to ankle in black oilskin. She peered closely through pebble-lenses into the porch of the Boatman and further along at the doorway of the yacht club. Gomer often homed in on licensed premises, redolent of the scent familiar to any who had lived in close proximity to the late Captain.

Gomer had been reared in the Tropics and had never ceased to be irritated as well as surprised by the northerly gusts that caught him in mid-flight between kitchen and greenhouse, whisking him seawards. True, he had developed a free-falling technique that facilitated a rapid if unnerving descent before the land gave out beneath him, but the experience was always upsetting as well as undignified.

'Go-mer!' Mrs Ogmore-Davies descended the steps that led from the old quay to the marina boardwalk and its berthing sprigs. It was still early in the season, but already most of the berths were occupied by bobbing, tall-masted sailing boats.

'Come, pretty. Come to Mammy, then. Go-mAAHH!' What the final exclamation lacked in musical quality, it made up for in volume. The sudden weakness in Mrs Ogmore-Davies's knees was not transmitted to her vocal cords. She had found Gomer—perched on the prow of a cabin cruiser and gazing quizzically at the contorted, sandalled but otherwise naked body of a man, draped across the foredeck of the same craft and apparently petrified in the act of crawling aft.

The torso of Gomer's macabre shipmate lay on its right side, chest exposed to Mrs Ogmore-Davies standing rooted to the boards. The head was turned away from her. The right arm was fully extended as though attempting to reach a handhold further along the deck. The left knee was bent up tight towards the stomach and covering the groin. Mrs Ogmore-Davies was later quite explicit on this point—and on one other. A thin wooden stake protruded from the victim's back in the vicinity of the left shoulder-blade. This she noted with a shudder when she stepped forward to scoop up Gomer. There was no blood—not to speak of or not that she could later remember—but then, if there had been any, it would surely have been dispersed and diluted by the rain on the deck. This last was to be Constable Lewin's theory up to the point where he ceased to accept the existence of a body at all.

It was the Constable who was to be next on the scene for, although Mrs Ogmore-Davies's scream was loud enough to wake the dead, it was mostly carried seawards by the wind, and those few of the living it roused from their slumbers assumed it to be the anguished cry of a seabird. Nor did Mrs Ogmore-Davies attempt to find assistance close at hand.

Idwel Pugh, the landlord of the Boatman, and his

stuck-up wife, lived on the premises, but they were the last people she would have turned to—especially with a nude man on her hands, dead or alive. She was panic-stricken, but she hadn't lost her reason. Nobody lived at the yacht club nor at any of the few other buildings along the harbour, so it was Dai Rees the Post she hurried to fetch from near the bridge. But Dai had long since continued his rounds along River Street, and it was the Constable Mrs Ogmore-Davies sighted at the door of the new police house he occupied, rent free, at the foot of the High Street.

'Come quick, *bach*,' she cried from across the road. 'There's a dead body. Murdered.'

'Go on,' said Lewin, more in irritation than rank disbelief. He had only come out to look at his daffodils while the kettle boiled. His police responsibilities didn't rightly start until eight o'clock; up to then, it was the County Force that was supposed to keep law and order. The sight of Mrs Ogmore-Davies with a parrot on her shoulder and sounding like the prophet of doom made an unpromising start to the day. 'Where is it, then?' He began buttoning up his tunic, the first slight indication that he was preparing for action.

'In the harbour. In a boat—STABBED to death.' The shouted emphasis caused Gomer to re-arrange himself on his perch. 'Are you coming or not?'

' 'Course I'm coming. Let me get my cap.' Constable Lewin went indoors reappearing a few moments later fully equipped for official business—or nearly. The drizzle had turned into quite heavy rain, so he went back for his rain-coat.

'Took long enough,' complained Mrs Ogmore-Davies, nearly running to keep up as the Constable strode out along the popple-stones. He was shorter than she was but half her age. He increased his pace.

'In my experience,' he observed gravely, 'dead bodies

don't go anywhere. Haste is no substitute for method, Mrs Ogmore-Davies. My wife is ringing the doctor.' He glanced down at his companion. 'You did take the pulse?'

'Pulse? What pulse? Didn't I tell you he's dead as mutton? Knew that as soon as I got there . . . before I got there,' Mrs Ogmore-Davies added darkly.

Lewin disregarded the last remark. There was no point in complicating police reports with references to the alleged psychic experiences of witnesses. He knew what Mrs Ogmore-Davies was leading up to and he had no intention of humouring that particular whim.

They reached the marina. 'There,' said Mrs Ogmore-Davies, pointing to the cabin cruiser a few yards ahead.

The constable stepped forward. 'Where?' he asked, staring at the empty deck. There was a moment's embarrassed silence.

'It was there five minutes ago,' Mrs Ogmore-Davies offered defensively. 'We should have been quicker getting here.'

Constable Lewin lifted his eyebrows. It was hardly necessary to point out the irrelevancy of time when discussing the disposition of a dead body. 'Nobody else saw it, then?'

'Gomer saw it, didn't you, my lovely?'

The policeman made a mental note definitely to include that observation in his report. 'Pity he can't tell us,' he commented wryly.

Mrs Ogmore-Davies hesitated. 'He doesn't talk.' Her lips tightened.

Gomer moved crab-wise along his owner's shoulder. 'Sod it,' he said, with perfect articulation.

CHAPTER 2

'One in four people have smelly feet. Well, bless my soul.'
Lord Grenwood, Chairman of Grenwood, Phipps the
well-known merchant bankers, treated each of his three
luncheon companions to a stare of undisguised appraisal.
'Never had problems in that direction, I'm happy to say.
Waterworks, now, that's an entirely different—'

'Not one in every four, Lord Grenwood.' Whatever
physiological confidence the aged banker had been about
to share was lost to the interruption from the big, earnest
American on his right. 'Statistics prove—'

'Almost anything, in my experience.' This time, the
interpolation came from the urbane Mark Treasure, Vice
Chairman of Grenwood, Phipps, who considered a discourse either on human olfactory problems in general or
Grenwood's prostate in particular as unpromising accom-
paniments to Dover sole. 'I doubt Rigley & Herbert
have needed to bother much about statistics over the
years,' Treasure added lightly. 'Or am I doing you an
injustice, Mr Crutt?' He smiled confidently at the fourth
member of the party.

Albert Crutt, Managing Director of Rigley & Herbert
Limited, manufacturing chemists and the makers of
Rigley's Patent Footbalm, shook his head in agreement.
He could do little else while coping with a mouthful of
gristle.

The Perceval Club in London's Pall Mall is celebrated
for many things—notably the number of distinguished if
superannuated politicians it counts among its members.
Culinary excellence has never been high on the Commit-
tee's list of priorities. The provision of a three-course
lunch at a price that does not make too large a hole in the

daily attendance allowance at the House of Lords is a pre-requisite for the majority of habitués.

Lord Grenwood invariably brought Americans to the Perceval in the usually erroneous belief that the vener-ability of the premises—matched by that of the mem-bers— was for them ample compensation for the short-comings of the chef. He applied the same principle to 'provincial visitors' which broadly covered anyone nor-mally domiciled north of Watford.

Edgar J. Crabthorne Jnr, President of the Hutstacker Chemical Corporation of West Virginia, seemed imper-vious to both the surroundings and the fare. He was noted for his impassivity and had not registered dismay even on being advised that tea was available only at tea-time.

The normally nervous, self-effacing and undersized Crutt was largely preoccupied with the various aspects of his personal and business predicament.

His train from South Wales had been late. There had been no taxis available at the station. He had completed the journey in a bus going the wrong way, by Under-ground and, finally, on foot—all in an unfamiliar city in pouring rain.

Since no London club of the gentlemanly kind sees fit to identify itself, ensuring thus that strangers need to enter in the role of grovelling supplicants, Crutt had been redirected by the hall porters of two such establishments before fetching up, wet and winded, at the right one.

Decades before as a student pharmacist morbid physi-ology had held him academically enthralled. There had been nothing academic about his drumming pulse, his uncoordinated knee movements or his steaming torso as he had floundered up the Perceval steps. He had tried to think of Bronwen who made it all worthwhile: in the cir-cumstances this only made it worse.

An urgent but hasty visit to the washroom had resulted in his jamming a generous portion of shirt in the open zip of his trousers — something neither remedied nor much improved by some frantic ministrations with a pair of nail scissors firmly attached to a washbasin by an inadequate length of stoutish chain.

The titled member who had come upon the hapless Crutt contorted over the basin, apparently performing one of several possible but unspeakable acts, had retreated immediately, consoled only by the conclusion that the fellow was unlikely to be British.

The same member was now eyeing Crutt suspiciously from across the dining-room, a circumstance that left no recourse but to swallow the gristle whole. Transferring the offending mouthful to his napkin would have nullified the usefulness of that linen square as cover for the gaping trouser front and frayed shirting beneath. Crutt had managed well enough standing at the bar and had marched stiffly to the table, one hand clasped across his lower stomach, in the manner of one about to throw up — as it happened, a common enough posture in the Perceval dining-room. Sitting down created entirely different problems. And he had yet to explain about the Judge.

Crutt took a large draught of not very good burgundy. 'We . . . we keep very careful sales figures, Mr Treasure,' he offered apologetically. 'It's never been company policy to commission . . . er . . .'

'Market research?' Treasure suggested helpfully.

'That's right.' Crutt nodded. 'Nor . . .'

'Nor retail audits, up-dated packaging, spin-off products, advertising or merchandising, or any other damn thing to put go in the business.' Edgar J. Crabthorne Jnr shook his head gravely.

'There was the aerosol version of the Footbalm. We introduced that seven years ago.' The tone was still apologetic. 'And we do a certain amount of advertising. Trade advertising, that is. But certainly we're very behind the times. We just have — '

'Seventy-two point four per cent of the UK market,' said Crabthorne in the tone of a Pope pronouncing on a heresy, and in his real capacity as a proprietor of Sweet-Feet Spray, a product that though regularly re-packaged, lavishly advertised, savagely merchandised and meticulously researched, had failed dismally to acquire a market share remotely approaching two digits.

'Our view has always been that extensive advertising tends to call attention to the product . . .'

Crabthorne regarded the speaker with the kind of interested amazement normally reserved by tolerant persons for those who contend the earth is flat.

'. . . and, of course, the condition,' Crutt continued earnestly. 'We feel sufferers are familiar enough with Rigley's Footbalm. Wider advertisement—to people in general, I mean—would be pointless and would only increase the embarrassment of requesting it.'

Lord Grenwood leant across the table. 'Like asking for French—'

'Quite so,' Treasure put in quickly and in deference to the susceptibilities of the craggy old female retainer, who, having brushed away the table crumbs, was now attempting to snatch up Crutt's napkin to go with the three she had already collected, but in the face of stern and inexplicable resistance from its temporary owner.

'I think you may have a point there, er . . . Albert.' said Crabthorne, who thought nothing of the sort, but who considered magnanimity would best serve his purpose. 'Maybe we can learn something from you people. Said so when you looked over our plant that time'—a reference to what for Crutt had been a totally bewildering experience two years earlier and which he was still doing his best to blot from his mind. 'Yes sir. You can surely teach us something about the British market,' Crabthorne added: there was no point in overdoing it. 'Once we get that merger through, with your know-how here and ours everywhere else, we can . . . er . . . we can really get going.'

The hesitation was justified. Crabthorne had firmly decided that if the so-called merger ever did get consummated the first person going anywhere would be Albert Crutt.

Sweet-Feet was only one range of products manufactured by the Hutstacker Chemical Corporation through its many factories across the world. Most of these products were market leaders. When Hutstackers met strong competition in any product area, the Corporation was usually powerful enough to beat it into second place by what it referred to as scientific marketing methods and the expenditure of a great deal of money. In the United Kingdom, Rigley's Footbalm had failed to be quelled by the scientific approach.

For nearly three years, Sweet-Feet had been subjected to every marketing strategy known to the Harvard Business School and other lesser centres of great learning. It had been re-packaged, re-priced and re-formulated. It had been the subject of qualitative and quantitative research, preceded by structured in-depth discussions, all of which had been considered useful at the time. Free samples had been mailed to a wide variety of peer group leaders in the potential user categories. These had included chiropodists, pedicurists, policemen and ramblers, most of whom had regarded the largesse as some kind of calculated insult. Due to an error, samples had also been sent to dog-breeders, one of whom had irritatingly reported excellent results in the deodorizing of wet Labradors.

Sweet-Feet was advertised seriously in the press, conspicuously on posters and humorously on television. In response to all this effort, the market for foot deodorants had expanded dramatically. Nothing much happened to the sales of Sweet-Feet, but Rigley's Footbalm had gone from strength to strength.

It was not in the nature of the Hutstacker Chemical Corporation to admit defeat. When it couldn't win in a selling situation, it adopted a new strategy: this it called creating a buying situation.

As financial advisers to Hutstacker's in Europe, the firm of Grenwood, Phipps had been briefed to purchase all the stock of the family-owned Rigley & Herbert at an irresistible price. What Crabthorne referred to as a merger was more accurately intended to be a take-over—submerger would have been more accurate still.

There were no Rigleys and only a few Herberts surviving as descendants of the nineteenth-century founders of the firm. Although shareholders, they were none of them engaged in the company, and all of them—save one— only too pleased to sell their interests for princely sums. Nor had they jointly considered it necesssary to employ expensive financial advisers to transmit this simple truth to Hutstacker's without delay, which was why Crutt had been nominated emissary. There remained the problem of the one Herbert who had so far proved unwilling to part with his holding.

The aged waitress retreated, grumbling under her breath. Crutt seemed temporarily more relaxed, napkin still in place. 'The Judge hasn't said no. On the other hand—'

'He hasn't said yes,' put in Treasure, reminded of a song. 'And with fifty-one per cent of the equity he can create—'

'A blocking situation,' pronounced Crabthorne portentously. 'I could see him myself.' He produced a complicated-looking diary. 'I'm not due in Paris till Monday.'

'If I may say so—' Crutt was sounding less confident— 'he doesn't . . . er . . .'

'Like Americans?' Crabthorne joked, attempting to

refold the diary whose concertina folds had got out of control.

'Lot of people don't,' Lord Grenwood volunteered dispassionately. 'Can't imagine why. My grandmother came from Boston. Perfectly decent woman. I remember . . .'

'It's not that' Crutt dared to interrupt not so much in the cause of Anglo-American amity as in the interests of fulfilling a firm obligation. 'He did most specifically state he was willing to discuss the matter with Mr Treasure and no one else.' Unthinkingly, he raised his napkin to wipe his glistening brow.

'Your fly's open,' Grenwood observed loudly enough to cause two passing members swiftly to glance downwards.

'And he wants me to go to him.' Treasure sounded less than enthusiastic.

Crutt was now doubly embarrassed. 'If you would be so good, Mr Treasure.' He fumbled beneath the table. 'He's writing to invite you. He said a night or two . . . the house is most comfortable and commodious, um . . .' His right arm gave a sudden jerk upwards and a beam of satisfaction appeared on his face.

'Got it done up have you?' enquired Grenwood. 'Tricky things, zips. Gone back to buttons myself,' he confided, more in the direction of the returned waitress than his luncheon companions. 'We'll have coffee in the smoking-room, Elsie.'

All four members of the party prepared to leave the cleared table. 'And the Judge lives in . . .?' Treasure asked as he rose.

'Panty,' declared the relieved Crutt boldly, and just before becoming aware, as he stood up, that the tablecloth was firmly attached to the top of his trousers.

The letter from His Honour Judge Henry Nott-Herbert arrived the following morning. Treasure wondered irreverently whether the Judge had journeyed through life having his name invariably mistaken for a protest. 'I'm Henry not Herbert' sounded like a promising first line for a music hall ditty.

The invitation was courteous and close to compulsive for a number of reasons. The writer explained that his advancing age and accompanying decrepitude made travelling burdensome. He went on that although a widower, he took pains to maintain a civilized abode and pleasure in having friends to stay in it. He was conscious of the need to treat 'the business matter' with due seriousness and would be especially grateful for the opportunity to debate the right thing to do with Treasure in person. A mutual friend had advised that Treasure's objectivity and discretion were legendary. Thus he would be deeply obliged if the banker and his talented wife would join him for as long as they cared to stay. Golf, sailing, walking and the fascinating cathedral at St David's were all agreeable distractions close at hand. In a postscript Judge Nott-Herbert had thought fit to add that he had just started on the Latour '61 and had no hesitation in declaring that Treasure would find it fit for drinking.

The banker promptly decided to accept the invitation — at least for himself. His wife, Molly, better known as Margaret Forbes the actress, was in a season at Chichester and much as she might have enjoyed a day or two in rural Wales, the point was academic.

Treasure welcomed the thought of a short and entirely justified business holiday. It was clear that the Judge, enfeebled by age, looked to him for independent counsel. This might be a trifle irregular in the circumstances, but wholly understandable. Like so many of the dwindling band of traditional merchant banks, Grenwood, Phipps had originally been engaged almost exclusively in arranging the disposition of private venture capital. Social and business evolution, plus the ravages of taxation, had drastically altered the reach of the business in recent times, but Treasure was well used to the role of professional counsellor to persons of immense wealth. The Grenwood family itself still constituted a major responsibility in this connection.

In his mind's eye, Treasure pictured Judge Nott-Herbert as someone not dissimilar to Lord Grenwood. Both were into their seventies and while — according to *Who's Who* — the Judge had not been born to exceptional riches, he was now on the way to acquiring them.

Treasure replied to the invitation in longhand, giving the day of his arrival and apologizing about his wife. He added lightly that the tennis elbow which temporarily prevented him from playing golf, happily did nothing to hinder his raising first growth claret to his lips, and that he looked forward to inspecting St David's.

As he handed the letter for posting to his secretary, the admirable Miss Gaunt, he speculated briefly on the likely identity of the unnamed mutual friend who had briefed the Judge so accurately on the lures that would fetch him to Wales.

There is no way of telling whether he would have been better or less pleased had he been aware that his calling as a banker was quite incidental to the Judge's purpose, and that the invitation had been prompted through knowledge of his reputation in a severely different guise.

CHAPTER 3

The man picked up the ringing 'phone in the untidy living-room. 'Two-four-two.'

'Morning, sir, Patton here.'

'Yes, Patton?'

'Suspect checked out half an hour ago, sir. I followed him to Paddington Station where he bought a first-class ticket to Fishguard. He boarded the nine o'clock through train at eight forty-five. He's wearing his clerical outfit sir.'

'Any baggage?'

'Largish suitcase. Doesn't look like he's coming back. Anything else sir?'

'No. Just make sure he leaves with the train. Then he's all ours. Thanks, Patton. We'll be in touch.'

Mark Treasure enjoyed railway stations, a characteristic common enough in those seldom obliged to use them.

The drive to West Wales, he had been advised, was long and boring. Panty was not on the railway, but could be reached quickly and comfortably by train to Fishguard Harbour, followed by a short cab ride. The idea of travelling on the Fishguard Express had been irresistible.

Paddington station had an especial attraction for the handsome and still hardly middle-aged banker. He paused on the main concourse unfashionably to gaze up at Brunel's mighty centre span. Several passers-by emulated his action, failed to recognize a mid-nineteenth century engineering feat of the first importance when they saw it, and hurried onwards; two confirmed their natural as well as untutored imperception by colliding with each other.

In his extreme youth, Treasure's infrequent visits to

London had begun and ended at this same station:
memories of innocent pleasures crowded back. As an
Oxford undergraduate the journeys here had been more
frequent and the pleasures usually less innocent. He gave
a half-smile at his own long, good-humoured visage
reflected in the glass of a telephone-box with a man in it:
the passage of years had not made him intolerant of
youthful exuberances—least of all his own youthful
exuberances. Wistfully, he recalled offering a proposal
of marriage while waiting for a London connection at
Didcot.

The 9 a.m. Fishguard train stood ready to be boarded
at Platform Five. True, it no longer oozed steam from
every joint, nor would it be hauled by a giant County
Class 4-6-0 locomotive in the green livery of the Great
Western, brightwork gleaming. Sadly, there was nothing
to indicate it was anything out of the ordinary.

No train out of Paddington had ever officially been
designated the *Fishguard* Express; all trains beyond
Swansea had been limited since the line opened. Indeed,
had it not been the last Friday in May, preceding the
Monday Spring Bank Holiday, this train would have gone
no further than Swansea, and Treasure would have had
to complete the journey by a local connection. Fishguard
no longer rated a regular through service. Yet for small
boys reared near wayside stations along the iron road to
West Wales, there had been no other name to apply to
the Irish boat-train that hurtled past, shaking the very
rafters of the toothy-eaved platform roofs and rumoured
to suck in Saturday train spotters who stood too near the
edge. Treasure had been such a boy. He had since visited
most parts of the world, but Fishguard—where he had
never been—was still, for him, a name redolent of
romance and adventure, his boyhood gateway to the west
and the unimaginable excitements that lay beyond. The
fact that what lay beyond was a slow boat to Rosslare and

a rather roundabout route to Dublin had never been material.

There was no hurry about boarding the train. Miss Gaunt had reserved a seat and also a place in the dining car. Pink, Treasure's equally dependable chauffeur, had somehow contrived to complete the journey from Chelsea to Paddington in fifteen minutes less than the half-hour they had allowed, despite the exigencies of the rush-hour traffic. The usually monosyllabic Pink had even boldly waxed eloquent on the speed of their passage as he had drawn up the Rolls in the station yard, by way of adding emphasis to his earlier observation that Treasure would be better served in doing the whole trip by road: Pink had relatives who kept a pub in St David's.

Treasure drifted towards a Menzies bookstall. It being Friday, he bought a copy of the *Spectator*. He hesitated over the *Economist*: although he was an occasional contributor, he decided to wait to be informed by the corporate copy on his return. He reached for the new Morris West.

'Would Mr Mark Treasure please report to the Manager's office.' The diction and the amplification of the message on the station's loudspeakers left something to be desired; Brunel could scarcely be blamed for the vagaries of variable input impedence. 'Would Mr Mark Treasure please . . .' There was no mistaking the summons the second time, and Treasure found himself preternaturally ruffled by the fact.

What could be the extent of the private disaster that warranted such public, indiscriminate pre-proclamation? He had talked to Molly on the telephone the night before: she had been well enough then. Had the silly girl—the adoring, adorable woman he couldn't live without—tripped over a cable or tumbled off a gantry in that gadgety barn of a theatre? Of course she hadn't; she would hardly be up yet. Then had her hotel taken fire? Where was the Station

Manager's office? And, in any case, shouldn't it be Station *Master*? On enquiring he discovered he was standing beside the place and a notice reading 'Area Manager'.

'My name's Treasure. You just broadcast . . .'

'Ah yes, Mr Treasure.' The young woman smiled brightly. Somehow he had expected to be confronted by an official in a frock coat and top hat, ready to impart bad tidings while preparing to see the Queen off to Windsor. The girl looked and sounded cheerful: it was bad news all right. 'We have a package for Judge Nott-Herbert.' She hesitated before continuing lightly. 'Sounds like a quotation, doesn't it. Judge not Herbert that ye be . . .'

'Quite so,' said Treasure, not too affably. He was relieved at the information, but daunted by the size of the parcel the girl pulled from the end of the counter that lay between them. It was about three feet long, like an oversized flower-box securely wrapped in brown paper and adhesive tape.

'The messenger said you'd be delivering it to the Judge in . . . er . . .' She glanced down at the label. 'In Panty, is it?'

'That's right. At least, I'm staying with him there. I didn't know about any parcel.' Treasure loathed carrying parcels. He already had a suitcase, a copy of the *Spectator* and the new Morris West. Was there no end to people's casual impositions. 'Is it heavy?'

'Just awkward.' The girl laughed. 'If you'd rather not take it, I'm sure we can arrange with the addressor to have it sent.' She examined the label again.

'Not at all,' said Treasure, mollified. After all, he was staying under the fellow's roof. 'Perhaps a porter . . . ?'

The girl looked grave. 'We don't have porters any more, I'm afraid. Or rather we can only lay them on at two days' notice. Silly, really, passengers are always complaining . . .'

The passenger she was addressing stifled the memory of

his own recent complaint that the railways were grossly overmanned. He grasped the parcel at what looked like the point of balance. 'Thank you very much. I'll take it.'

'If you could sign here, sir?'

The First Class compartment in which Treasure's place was reserved already had five of its six seats occupied by other travellers, one of them a small boy wielding a skateboard and in the charge of an indulgent-looking female. Treasure decided to give it a miss.

It was obviously British Rail's practice to connote foresight with gregariousness and to crowd together all those sensible enough to reserve seats in as few compartments as possible.

Treasure found a whole unreserved carriage—the second from the engine—that at first sight seemed hardly occupied. On closer inspection, each compartment proved to contain one or two passengers. He chose one whose single occupant was a clergyman dozing in a window seat. He enjoyed the company of clergy. He did not enjoy imagining he looked like a refugee hung about with household chattels done up in brown paper parcels. In truth, he was unmistakably an affluent citizen in well cut tweeds, carrying a suitcase and one neat package.

He closed the door from the corridor and distributed his impedimenta on the overhead racks on both sides, before taking the seat diagonally opposite the cleric. He stole a glance at his travelling companion—a large and muscular man, with a shock of white hair and a moustache which at first sight had belied his age: Treasure now put this at no more than forty.

'Good morning.' The clergyman's eyes opened swiftly and in time disarmingly to catch Treasure's appraising gaze. 'You're braver than most of your compatriots.' The tone was deep: the accent distinctly Antipodean.

'Good morning.' Treasure replied. He smiled. 'I'm not

sure I follow your meaning.'

'It's my experience a dog collar scares people off.'

'Some people, perhaps, and I doubt if it's much different down under. You from New Zealand?'

'Sydney, Australia, but that's the gentlemanly way to find out.'

Treasure chuckled. 'I've never understood why New Zealanders are so outraged if they're mistaken for Australians. In any case, I shouldn't have assumed irrational susceptibilities in a clergyman. You an Anglican?' The other man nodded after a just perceptible moment of hesitation. 'My name's Treasure, by the way. The Church of England in Australia,' he added after a pause. 'I've always thought that a rather ponderous title and inappropriate, in a way, since you could drop both our provinces into any one of your four—'

'And still leave room for the sheep.' The cleric had interrupted before Treasure had time to correct himself. The man glanced at his watch and then picked up a copy of *The Times* from the seat beside him, perhaps to indicate that the conversation had run its course.

Treasure cleared his throat. 'I met the Bishop of Victoria last year in Melbourne. Nice man . . . huh, name's gone out of my head.'

'Is that so.' Treasure's putative question had been ignored as he had suspected it might be, and not simply because the Australian church had five provinces nor even because there was no Bishop of Victoria.

The banker had a very large number of friends in holy orders, some of them luminaries, some of them quite well off, but he could not think of one who, in addition to travelling First Class, wearing handmade shoes, a Savile Row suit, a platinum wristwatch and a well-fitting wig, would also sport what to a tutored observer was a just perceptibly false moustache. Treasure accepted that there were any number of affluent clergy who might have trouble passing through the eye of the proverbial needle and that these might well include some who preferred to disguise premature baldness. It was only the moustache that raised doubt and probably irrational suspicion in the mind of one accustomed to expect total probity in clergymen and given to seeking out any shortcoming that made an actor's performance less than flawless.

Treasure's deepening curiosity about his fellow traveller was not to be assuaged. After a further short exchange of pleasantries, the wealthy cleric had taken refuge behind his newspaper, and later occupied himself with a book. Although Treasure had volunteered his own name, the other man had deftly avoided offering his and indeed any further information about himself, save that he was on holiday. Three hours later, he declined Treasure's invitation to join him for lunch and, as the banker moved along the train in the direction of the dining car, he reflected that he might have fallen in with a mountebank in the habit of harmlessly disguising himself as a clergyman for the express purpose of preserving his privacy on railway trains and who, on this occasion, had allowed his enthusiasm to run away with him.

This amusing speculation occurred to Treasure again as he was returning to his compartment after consuming an unexpectedly agreeable plate of steak and kidney pie washed down by a passable half-bottle of claret, albeit at a fairly early hour, and an accelerated pace. He had barely had time to consume his coffee before the table was unceremoniously denuded of everything save the bill. There being few objects so depressingly bare as an unclothed restaurant-car table top, Treasure had decided to take the hint and remove himself. Lunch had begun compulsorily at twelve-thirty. It was now only a little after one-fifteen: an early finish which was later to assume some significance. At the time it had compounded irritation. He had taken his suitcase and what he thought had been all his other belongings to the diner, believing the train might reach its destination while he was still there. He had forgotten the Judge's parcel until half way through the meal. Thus he had had to carry his bag both ways to no purpose.

The train had stopped at Llanelli, on schedule, and Treasure wondered idly whether the Australian had alighted there at what was an unlikely holiday resort. Although famous for its steel industry, Llanelli happened also to be the home of Rigley & Herbert Ltd. Albert Crutt was no doubt somewhere close by, unwittingly confounding the onward march of modern marketing, while continuing to bank the growing profits of Rigley's Patent Footbalm.

It was as the banker negotiated the swaying concertina tunnel that led to the corridor of the carriage next to his own that he heard the sharp crack of the explosion. It was a common enough railway noise, and consistent with the bang given off by the warning devices fixed to the line when track repairs are in progress. The train was crossing points prior to entering Whitland Station—a minor junction, but a popular stopping place, judging by the numbers of passengers with baggage in the corridor waiting to get off.

The explosion registered only momentarily with Treasure as he concentrated on keeping his balance and attempted to find his way around the press of people. Since this was as difficult as it was pointless, he decided to wait in the corridor.

Whitland Station disappointed. It was not a characterful country junction with bits of shining brasswork, iron-cast cautionary notices, and flower-beds on the platforms. It was modern and grey with a prefabricated look to all its adjuncts, purposefully arranged for the needs of holiday-makers and others en route to the seaside area served by its branch line.

Numbers of passengers having now disgorged themselves on to the platform, Treasure made to proceed
through to the corridor of his own carriage. To his surprise, the connecting door was locked: not simply stuck
but immovably secured.

The guard was blowing his whistle from the rear of the
train. Although this was intended as a signal to the
driver, departure was not imminent since some carriage
doors were still standing open: even so, officials were
making some haste to close them.

'I can't get through to the next carriage.' Treasure
addressed the uniformed man with the cheerful countenance who was just about to slam the door in front of
him. 'The door's locked. Could you open it, please?'

'Can't be locked, sir. Must be stuck. This way then.
Have to be quick, like.'

The official grabbed Treasure's case, and taking him
by the arm, bundled bag and passenger on to the platform and in again through the door of the next carriage.
He slammed both doors as the train moved off. 'All right?'
he mimed amiably through the glass, nodding self-
approval, and stood back from the train wearing the
triumphant expression of an old hand who had proved yet
again that where there's a will there's a way.

Treasure remained unconvinced that the door in
question was merely stuck and not locked unofficially by
someone for whom a locked door would, at this stage in
the journey, save work while only inconveniencing passengers. This was an uncharitable and unsupported conclusion, but it fitted with the times—like grey railway
stations. He tried the door. It felt to be as firmly locked as
it had from the other side.

He moved along the corridor, noting that the three
compartments he had to pass before reaching his own
were now completely empty. At first sight it appeared the
fourth one was also. As he slid open the door he glanced

involuntarily upwards at the luggage rack. The Judge's parcel had gone, as had the clergyman's case. The disquiet thus sparked was to be quickly increased.

The Australian clergyman was struggling to lift himself from the floor of the compartment. He had one hand to his forehead. Thin rivulets of blood were escaping between the fingers. What Treasure could see of the top half of the face was smudged with black. There was an acrid smell in the air.

The banker heaved the stricken man on to the nearest seat. 'Tell me what's happened. Are you badly hurt?'

Despite first appearances, the victim seemed more dazed than physically injured. Treasure moved the man's hand away from his forehead, revealing a wide but not deeply scarred area of bloody skin. This was framed with smears of the black substance which had mingled with the blood. The shock of white hair was not so much disturbed as relocated. Incongruously it had moved backwards and sideways, revealing here and there a kind of underthatch of short brown stubble: it was also singed at what should have been the front but which now roughly surmounted the wearer's right ear.

'The bastards tried to shoot me.' It was an excusable enough statement in the circumstances whatever the speaker's calling. 'Right in my face . . . but godammit they missed.'

The incongruities were now coming thick and fast. The clergyman's accent had undergone a fundamental change.

'If you can look after yourself for a minute, I'm going to get help.' Treasure was not clear from where help might be forthcoming, but the consoling offer seemed appropriate. 'D'you have a clean handkerchief for your forehead?' He was reluctant to part with one of his own unless it was entirely necessary: it was not, and the man was beginning to come out of his daze.

'I'm OK . . . OK . . . the grip.' He glanced upwards as he began applying the handkerchief to his brow. 'They stole my grip, the crazy goons . . . two guys . . . got away back there.' He pointed not very accurately in the general direction of Whitland Station.

Treasure was reminded that on the evidence he had also been relieved of some baggage. 'Right,' he said firmly, 'hold tight, I'm stopping the train.'

The victim nodded. His companion reached across the carriage to succumb to one of life's most resisted but familiar temptations. Grasping the communication cord he pulled down hard, noting fleetingly the printed stricture that the penalty for improper use had been increased to £50.

With much grinding and jolting, the train came dramatically to a halt.

CHAPTER 4

Treasure had established the carriage was empty except for himself and the afflicted cleric: it was also locked at both ends. There being no alternative, he had opened an outside door and dropped down awkwardly to the track. There was no logical reason why he had chosen to complete this manoeuvre with suitcase in hand, but thus encumbered he set off at a brisk pace towards the rear of the train. Whitland Station he judged to be about three hundred yards beyond.

Few windows were opened because few train windows are now made to open. Treasure was treated to glances through fixed glass: without instruction, most viewers were deeply inured to the concept of waiting for normal service to be resumed.

Treasure had hoped for human contact with someone who without the need for delaying explanation could be despatched to tend the assaulted: none such appeared. The dining-car staff was having its lunch as planned— undisturbed by customers and to all appearances unaware the train had stopped. A small boy—the one with the skateboard—was standing on a corridor window-ledge, his head thrust through the narrow aperture of a ventilation window. 'Mummy,' he called, probably ineffectively, 'It's a man who's missed the station.'

The guard was firmly of the same opinion. ' 'Ere,' explained that worthy as Treasure drew within hailing distance of his van. ' 'Ere, did you stop this train? You can't . . .'

'A clergyman has been shot in the second carriage from the front.' Treasure had halted before the open door of the guard's van, the better to impress the import of his message: he was also keen to lighten his burden. 'Look after this will you?' He put down his suitcase. 'Get someone to take care of the parson. I'm going for a doctor and the police.'

There was no purpose in further explanation although it was clear the guard meant to demand some. Treasure made off at a creditable jog. It was three or four minutes since the train had pulled away from Whitland.

As he approached the concrete gradient leading up to the platform, it became obvious that the business part of the station was opposite, on the up platform. The main buildings were there, and behind them he could make out a narrow, sloping yard with cars parked. On the down platform there was only a siding and a coal yard. The station had an overhead footbridge and beyond that a level-crossing with the gates now closed to trains and very much open to traffic and pedestrians. It seemed the station was near the centre of town. Treasure crossed the line.

'What are you doing here?' The cheerful uniformed figure encountered earlier was advancing from the booking hall. Here at least was someone aware that this particular passenger had not intended to alight at Whitland.

The breathless Treasure slowed his pace but kept moving firmly towards the likely site of telephones and departing miscreants. Having no option, the official fell in beside him.

'Attempted murder on the train. Need a doctor and the police. See anyone with a long parcel?'

'Murder, is it? *Duw, Duw.*' The official was impresssed. 'Make way,' he called ahead to the knot of people at the ticket-barrier. 'Bert, see anyone with a long parcel?'

The ticket-collector looked up from filling out an excess journey ticket. 'Yes, him . . . them, and they haven't got tickets either . . .'

Treasure inwardly froze. The two young men indicated

by the ticket-collector's nod were standing brazenly just inside the glazed booking hall waiting—incredibly—to pay their excess fare. One was holding a leather case that Treasure instantly recognized as belonging to the clergyman. The other was clutching the Judge's unmistakable parcel.

The two gave every appearance of being social dropouts, at least against the standards applied by merchant bankers. Both were dresssed over-all in blue denim. It was not debatably fashionable worn and torn denim but repulsively genuine worn, torn and very dirty denim. Both had hair that was long, unkempt and matted, as well as wispy beards that promised to be the same given time to develop. They wore large and rimless dark glasses in the manner of those who do so perversely not to keep out sunlight but to stay in night light. They were sockless and sandalled. They looked undernourished, determinably underprivileged and surprisingly unconcerned.

'Call the police.' Treasure hoped this loud injunction would be heard and acted upon by someone in the ticket-office. 'That luggage doesn't belong to you,' he continued in a quieter but firm tone, 'and that's not all you need to explain.'

'Attempted murder, is it?' Treasure had not intended to enlarge on his statement. The shocked station official did so for him with no regard for the laws of libel nor the likely effect of such a pronouncement upon innocent on-lookers, who promptly dispersed in all directions, leaving the banker, the official and the ticket-collector to act out any heroics necessary.

It was at this point that the guard from the train arrived as unintended reinforcement for the powers of goodness, and carrying Treasure's suitcase. 'He's stopped the bloody train . . .' he began, outraged, levelling an accusing arm at the banker.

'Cool it, Dad.' The flaxen-haired youth with the parcel

stared contemptuously at Treasure. 'Just everybody stay loose, and no one gets hurt.' Casually he withdrew a Service-type revolver from inside his shirt. The guard's mouth dropped open. 'Now, we got a car outside. We're gonna get in it, an' we're gonna drive away peaceful . . .'

Mr Ifor Beynon—the powerfully built ex-Sergeant Beynon, DCM, long since retired from the Welsh Guards—had entered the booking hall earlier from the station yard to collect a consignment of homing pigeons timed for release at two o'clock. In the interim he had found the wicker basket containing his temporary charges, where the goods clerk usually placed them in a privileged position just inside the entrance. He had also witnessed the whole exchange at the ticket-barrier.

The commendation that had accompanied Sergeant Beynon's Distinguished Conduct Medal stated that he had demonstrated initiative as well as bravery under fire. That had been forty years ago: his spirit and instinct had not dimmed with time. With his right foot he slammed shut the heavy glass door behind him. Simultaneously he slipped the fastening on the wicker basket and threw back the lid.

Though normally mild enough creatures, racing pigeons offered freedom after hours of confinement and a crowded train journey are far from docile. The twenty-five birds released by Mr Beynon had one object in common—to return to Uxbridge by the quickest possible route. Freedom beckoned only from the other side of the ticket-barrier.

Twenty-five excited, healthy, competitive pigeons took to the air behaving like oversized bats in an undersized belfry. Their wings beat against the walls and ceiling of the tiny booking hall. They collided with each other and all else that obstructed. They swooped, they glided, they circled and they squawked. But mostly they harassed the two terrified youths whom they had taken so unexpectedly from the rear and who were filling most of the available space at the only point of exit.

The villains were instantly transformed into victims. They ducked and weaved and thrashed with their arms. The one with the gun beat the air around his head as half-a-dozen winged persecutors scratched and clawed at his scalp and neck. He turned about, shielding his eyes with his forearm, only to have another predator fly into his open shirtfront and make heavy going of getting out again.

The second youth had lost his glasses and his nerve. 'Shoot the bastards!' he screamed. The gun went off — a noise not unfamiliar to the pigeons whose trained desire to head for home was now intensified by a quickening of the instinct to do with self-preservation; their panic quickened too.

The beleaguered youth fired the gun again, and again, and again . . .

The ticket-collector had disappeared from view behind the protecting counter-front of his booth. The guard had taken refuge in a doorway, still clutching the suitcase. The station official and Treasure pressed themselves flat against the wall on the platform. And Treasure was counting. His knowledge of firearms was limited but he believed most revolvers held six rounds. One shot had done for the clergyman. Five more had just exploded inside the booking hall. Unless the youth had reloaded . . . Immediately after the fifth shot rang out, there was the unmistakable click of a firing pin working against an empty chamber.

Mr Beynon was no layman when it came to firearms. He had been waiting for a sixth shot, but acted on the altogether recognizable, audible evidence that the gun was empty. He picked up the wicker basket and bellowing 'Now!' charged with it across the booking hall.

A flailing, confused mass of birds, men and possessions

disgorged on to the platform followed by a triumphant Mr Beynon, now struggling with the basket at the door. 'Get the blond one, sir,' he shouted at Treasure.

Already the two youths were on their feet. 'Over the line, Ken,' screamed Treasure's designated quarry, who still had the parcel in his grasp—and an empty revolver in one hand. He blundered backwards towards the platform edge, less bothered by birds but with his earlier *sang-froid* totally shattered. His companion, adopting a crouched position, also began retreating. He wielded the suitcase in front of him to keep the advancing station official at bay—and succeeded in clouting that plucky assailant painfully across both knees with the improvised weapon.

Mr Beynon's charge had been halted when the basket stuck firmly in the doorway. He now struggled with it on to the platform, and, despite his seventy years, hurled this bulky missile at the second youth, launching himself after it intending to flatten his quarry. But the enemy was too quick: he fended back the basket in time for Mr Beynon to trip over it and to come down heavily, well short of target.

Treasure meantime rashly attempted a high rugby tackle, hoping to floor his encumbered opponent before he could quit the platform. This was a mistake. Although the skinny youth had the pallid look of one permanently excused all games from an early age, he was just as evidently the sort who didn't play—or fight—according to anybody's rules. He met Treasure's approach with a swift, accurate and powerful kick to the groin.

'You won't get away,' shouted the station official without much conviction. 'Oh, my sainted knee,' he added from the sitting position.

The two fugitives scrambled down to the railway line, leaving the attack force in temporary disarray—except for the guard who now came fresh to the fight from the shelter of the doorway. From his towering vantage point on the platform edge he swung Treasure's suitcase at the man called Ken, in time for it to catch him with powerful force behind the left ear, sending him sprawling across the rails. The victim gave a cry of pain, clasping both hands to his head and releasing the case in his charge. His companion, although already started across the track, turned back in what seemed at first to be a comradely act of succour until it became obvious he was seeking to retrieve the suitcase.

Mr Beynon, with a twisted ankle, was by this time hopping manfully to the platform edge on one leg. The station official was still down, and the guard—a man not over-endowed with a sense of the courageous—was standing irresolute, proud that his single contribution to the fight might have decisive effect, but with both assailants out of reach, not anxious to mix with them at rail level.

Treasure was upright, but in extreme pain. The blond youth was now just below him trying to dislodge the clergyman's suitcase which had become stuck between platform base and rail. The banker made a grab at the only hand-hold on offer—the corner of the long parcel. The enemy resisted being thus dispossessed with one arm while wrenching the suitcase free with the other.

The second youth was now unsteadily on his feet. 'Take this and run!' shouted the blond, heaving the case into the centre of the track before applying his full strength and attention to the bizarre tug of war with Treasure and the parcel. Already the outer wrappings of the thing were beginning to disintegrate, uncovering a cardboard box beneath. Treasure was pulling at the lower edges. His opponent had hold of the top which, in response to a violent tug, suddenly slid off in his hands. At the same moment, Treasure gave his end of the box a twist—with unnerving effect.

Out popped a hideous, shrunken, hairy head with a painted face fixed in a ghoulish grin.

Treasure released the box with a shudder and so abruptly that he fell backwards on to Mr Benyon. The blond youth gave a whoop of triumph.

'Get off the line! For God's sake, get off the line!' It was the station official who shouted the warning.

The 13.04 up-train to London, running over fifteen minutes late, was pounding in to Whitland, its driver intent on making up time. The train was still travelling at twenty miles an hour when it passed the western end of the station. There was distance enough for the driver to halt the twelve carriages at the prescribed point but not allowing for the survival of persons unlawfully disporting themselves on the line in front of the booking hall.

'Look out!' Treasure shouted involuntarily at the two men with whom, moments before, he had been engaging in mortal combat.

Each man dropped what he was carrying and leapt for the opposite track—as it seemed to the brief glimpse allowed those on the platform—directly under the rear wheels of the Fishguard train which, unseen by the combatants, had been quietly backing in to the station.

It went through Treasure's mind that no matter how slowly the reversing train was moving, it could not be remotely inhibited by human beings in its path.

CHAPTER 5

'Miraculous escape. That's what the papers will say. And there's another one.' Detective-Inspector Glyn Iffley stamped on the brake pedal of the decrepit-looking Mini Estate. The car halted a few inches short of an aged Whitland resident exercising his undoubted right to risk his life with minimum notice at the last pedestrian crossing on the edge of town. 'You comfy?' The pedestrian was proceeding without haste and any expression of appreciation.

If there was comfort in the knowledge that the final lap of an unwarrantably adventurous, painful and protracted journey had actually begun, then Treasure could answer in the affirmative. Even so, the vehicle in which he was travelling, though mechanically sound, seemed not to have been fashioned — or re-fashioned — to ensure that passengers rode in it at their ease: no matter, he was on his way again: it was three-thirty.

More than two hours before, Treasure and his faithful retainer, the station official, had been among the first to arrive on the down platform of Whitland Station to search for the run-over remains of their erstwhile adversaries. It was not until a passenger positively witnessed that two men had made off through the coal yard bordering the platform that the unrelished quest had been abandoned.

Meantime, help had arrived in the rough but ready balance of one police car, three fire-engines, six ambulances and an ice-cream van. Large numbers of townspeople had followed in the wake of this little armada, joining a crush of de-training and mostly disgruntled passengers in and around the station.

For a while, stretchers and wheelchairs had been much

in evidence until it became apparent that no one needed them—saving only Mr Beynon, who after protest had consented to be wheeled from the scene after establishing there had been no fatalities among the pigeons.

The first policemen to appear—a sergeant and a constable—had needed to organize the pursuit of the long-departed villains as well as to establish order in general. Treasure had been patient, but after the arrival of a larger police contingent he had insisted that the sergeant accompany him to the front of the train where he had already despatched two ambulance men to tend the wounded cleric.

It had been irritating and embarrassing next to discover that there was no wounded cleric. The sergeant and the ambulance men had accepted Treasure's word for it that a clergyman had existed. The guard who had re-attached himself to Treasure's entourage at this point of non-discovery had been darkly and purposefully sceptical.

The criminal intentions of the two fugitives had been well enough established by their conduct on Whitland Station. That they had earlier assaulted a passenger causing Treasure to stop the train was a matter for conjecture so far as the guard was concerned. He had already been mentally composing his forthcoming written report on irregularities as heinous as the incidence of locked corridor doors and his literally unguarded abandonment of a stationary but re-mobilized train. Others, no doubt, would report he had contributed little to arresting an affray on railway property, beyond providing porterage for the luggage of a public-spirited passenger.

What had happened at Whitland Station would not have involved the Fishguard train at all if it had not been stopped by Treasure in the first place. The guard believed the absence of a battered clergyman put him well on the way to confusing the deliberations of any enquiring body out to blame him for anything.

It had been Detective-Inspector Iffley who, with the uniformed sergeant, had examined the corridor toilet. The washbasin had been liberally anointed with splashings of what looked like blood, charcoal and mixings of both. A copious length of roller towel unhitched from its cabinet had been stained with the same substances. The inspector had ordered samples to be taken for analysis. He had offered that there seemed no doubt that Treasure's cleric had used the place to clean up before disappearing.

Iffley had thus endeared himself to the banker almost from the time of his arrival. A natural respect for a senior police officer might have been instantly manifest had it not been for the fellow's unconventional appearance and laconic disposition.

Iffley was a large, genial man, thirty or so, a bit overweight, with curly, light brown hair, a freckled, innocent face and a pleasing baritone voice. He was dressed in faded red linen trousers, worn blue canvas shoes, and a whitish T-shirt emblazoned with the message 'Get it together with Tia-Maria'. It had been the unpoliceman-like garb that initially gave Treasure pause — as it had the uniformed officers present when the Inspector had first appeared. Even so, having diffidently established his seniority, the man had quietly but firmly taken charge.

The Mini was now moving westwards again with an alacrity and smoothness that belied its appearance. It occurred to Treasure that this description fitted both car and owner. 'Shall you remain in charge of the hunt and . . . er, the enquiry, Inspector?'

'No, sir, thank the Lord. I've handed over to the chap who arrived from Carmarthen.' The policeman chuckled. 'Didn't look very pleased with life, did he. He was expecting to be off duty for the long weekend after lunch today. No rest for the wicked in this job.'

'But what about you . . . ?'

'Oh, I just happened to be the nearest ranking copper and got flagged down by this thing.' Iffley pointed to the radio. 'It's two-way.'

'Indeed.' The equipment had a discarded look. Treasure now noticed it included a microphone. 'So this *is* a police car. I mean, it's not your own . . .'

'Banger? No, sir. And it goes like the clappers, too. It's just that I have to cultivate an uncared-for look in my business.' The speaker paused, and then ahead of Treasure's question, continued. 'I'm with a Regional Crime Squad in another area, seconded here on special assignment.'

'Sounds very cloak and dagger.'

'In a way, sir. There was a big drug haul here . . .'

'I remember,' Treasure cut in. 'Headline stuff at the time. But I thought you'd nabbed everybody involved?'

'We did, or rather the coppers on the job did. I wasn't one of them. New face. Got put in later to look for stragglers. Been living around the hippy communes in them there hills.' Iffley nodded in the direction of the undulating grasslands to the north of the road.

'This is commune country?'

'Mm, California without the sun . . . or the smog, I suppose. People shiftless, shifty, and shifting, someone said. Right, too. They're all imports, of course. Bloody English drop-outs and junkies, most of 'em.' The policeman glanced sideways to judge Treasure's reaction. Both men smiled. 'Welsh myself, though not so's you'd notice any more, I suppose.'

'So am I mostly. Wales is a good place to be from, though.' Treasure had less claim to evident Welsh affiliations than his companion whose accent was fairly pronounced. 'Have you done any good here?'

'Difficult to say, sir.' The speaker paused either to concentrate on passing the car and caravan ahead or else to avoid answering the question. The driving manoeuvre was accomplished with an astonishing burst of acceleration. Iffley then reduced the speed of the little car in token acknowledgement at entering a built-up area. They were passing through the village of Commercial or *Llanddewivelfey*.

Treasure had already noted that the traditional English place names along the route were everywhere offered on new road signs incorporating Welsh alternatives as well. As a conscientious banker he knew the Welsh for commercial was *masnachol*, even though he was not quite sure how to pronounce it. There was no evidence of commercial activity save for the sale of petrol. Perhaps the little community had taken the opportunity to acquire a vernacular name more mellifluous and appropriate than the old English one.

'I was interested in your two villains. If we don't catch 'em straight away, I may be able to identify them, or else get them identified.'

'You mean they'll belong to your hill people, Inspector?'

'Very possibly, and almost certainly on drugs, sir, both of them fairly high, too, at the time you were dealing with them.'

Treasure nodded. 'At the start they were terribly relaxed . . .'

'Paying their excess fare.' The policeman chuckled. 'That fits well enough. Either they were working on their own hoping to steal the cost of a few fixes or else they were employed to do a specific job.'

'I think the latter, don't you? They had a car, a gun, they seemed to know what they were after, and they weren't a bit keen to let it go.'

'Possibly.' Iffley seemed to be thinking aloud. 'I don't think there was a car. I mean, we believe we accounted for all the cars in the yard. On the other hand, the gun probably doesn't belong to them. If it did, they'd have sold it rather than use it to frighten people.'

'They did more than frighten the clergyman.'

'But they were using blanks throughout. Of course you can do a lot of superficial damage with a blank cartridge fired close to, especially a .45.' Iffley paused, clicking his tongue against his lower lip. 'We know they got on the train at Llanelli because all tickets were inspected earlier between Swansea and Llanelli.'

'I know, I was in the dining car.'

'If they were hired they were probably given the money for the fare.' The Inspector still appeared to be communing with himself. 'In which case, having dodged buying tickets in the first place, they'd have been anxious not to have a fuss made when they failed to slip through without paying at Whitland. Could have got them into trouble with whoever's paying them.'

'Dishonesty's often a false economy.' Treasure felt this a suitable reflection to offer a policeman. 'Anyway, they ended up looking pretty conspicuous. Beats me how they got away with the business on the train. I mean, the clergyman could have recovered enough to raise hell before they were clear, or someone else could have got on. Imagine taking that kind of risk.'

Iffley shook his head. 'Nothing out of the way for some of the mindless zombies I consort with, sir. They probably thought they'd done for the parson . . .'

'Killed him, you mean? But . . .'

'It's quite possible they thought they were using real ammo, and if they were hired for the job, and if the price was high enough, that wouldn't have bothered them one bit.'

'Good God.' Treasure had imagined life in rural West Wales to be fairly sheltered compared even to the King's Road, Chelsea.

'The whole thing would have been a giggle.'

'That's exactly how they were behaving when I caught up with them.'

'Anyway, it would have taken the parson a bit of time to come round . . . the shock apart from anything else, sir. Would depend on his age, of course.' There was disappointment in the tone: Treasure had felt unable to guess the victim's age with real accuracy. 'As for other passengers, the ticket-collector said there never are any first-class passengers getting on at Whitland for Fish-guard. A lot get off — to change trains. Hardly anybody gets on. The only other first-class ticket holders still on the train were you and people in reserved seats in the next carriage.'

A twinge of pain in the lower stomach reminded Treasure that if he had been prepared to suffer little children he too could have travelled in a reserved seat, untroubled, unmolested and delivered on time to his destination. Instead he was bravely bearing the hurt of behaving like a responsible citizen — far from convinced by the light-hearted assurances of a Whitland doctor that no permanent damage had been done to some of the more delicate parts of his anatomy: time would tell.

'Sad about your little man, sir.'

The banker, roused from self-pity, was astonished at what seemed a flippant descent into nursery metaphor. But Iffley was snatching a brief glance at the assorted objects in the rear of the car.

'Ah, you mean the ventriloquist's doll? I don't suppose the Judge is going to be very pleased about its condition.'

Iffley smirked. 'Expect it looked better before the train ran over it, sir.'

'Not much, actually. Gave me a hell of a shock.' Treasure turned properly to view the casualty where it lay on view in the bottom of its box — the only surviving piece of the original elaborate wrapping. On reflection, perhaps the thing was being maligned.

Viewed without the drama of its first exposure, the doll was obviously intended to amuse. Far from being a horrifying sort of doll, it bore a marked resemblance to Stan Laurel, the slim member of the old-time film comedy partnership of Laurel and Hardy. Taking its adventures into account, the doll had survived mostly unscathed. it had evidently not been run over: only fought over. A plastic bag of extra properties was attached to its left leg: this included a bowler hat with wire attachments. Treasure had discovered that a ventriloquist's doll was an altogether more intricate mechanical contrivance than he had conceived before becoming closely involved with one.

'Not something anyone would try stealing. Not knowingly.' This was the policeman. 'Might be valuable, but imagine trying to fence it—sell it off as stolen property.' The last definition had been unnecessary. Not for the first time, Treasure noted a tendency among youngish policemen to treat bankers like members of the judiciary.

'This is Haverfordwest, sir. Old county town.' The car had crossed a river bridge and with power to spare was effortlessly ascending a monstrously steep hill and still evidently Georgian High Street.

'Named by Danish raiders, settled by Flemish weavers, and held for King Charles for a bit in the Civil War. I expect you know.' Treasure catechized his last evening's homework purposefully with an air of easy scholarship. 'Unless I'm mistaken'—an unlikely possibility—'that's St Mary's—thirteenth and fifteenth century, and reputed to be the finest church in the whole of southern Wales. Nice clock.' He was good at churches, and planned to visit the one they had just speeded past as soon as it became convenient. Meantime he recalled: 'They didn't steal the clergyman's watch. I noticed it particularly. Platinum, I think. But it did look as if they'd turned out his pockets, as I told you.'

The western outskirts of Haverfordwest didn't merit

comment, and Treasure was anxious to spend his remaining time with the policeman to the best purpose. A roadsign announced, 'Solva 11, Panty 13, St David's 15'.

'They might have thought it was stainless steel, sir.'

It went through Treasure's mind that any kind of watch might be acceptable to someone intent on stealing 'the cost of a few fixes'—fitting one of the Inspector's own speculations.

'You mean they thought the jackpot would be in the suitcase? Was it?' The banker put the question casually. In fact, he was very intrigued to know if the contents of the case had proved as curious as their owner.

'Not really, sir.' Iffley was not to be drawn. The momentary pause in the conversation accentuated the point. 'Are you staying long with the Judge, sir?'

'A few days only.' Treasure sensed and respected the professional reticence that had ordered the change of subject. 'Are you sure I'm not taking you out of your way . . . or blowing your cover?' He was getting his own back for the definition of 'fence'.

'The answer's no in both cases, sir. I have to take this route and we reckon my cover as a not very clewed-up antique-buyer is blown already. Anyway, I'm being withdrawn. Just going down to tidy up.'

'I wouldn't have thought there were many antiques left for buying in this part of the world.'

'Dead right. The area was picked pretty clean years ago. By professionals, too. I make out I'm after lower grade bric-à-brac.' Iffley shrugged his ample shoulders. 'Just so I have, or used to have, excuse to poke round the farms and cottages. Of course,' he added a shade defensively, 'you can come across a bit of art nouveau now and again. That's worth a quid or two these days.'

It would have been tactless to confirm that the Inspector looked more like a junk merchant than a senior policeman. Treasure concluded also it would be impertinent—if potentially profitable—to enquire whether Iffley had disposed of the better *objets d'art* that had come his way. Molly Treasure had a nose for acquiring pieces of yesterday's junk destined to become tomorrow's four-figure saleroom items: her husband had learned to foster and fuel her enterprise at every opportunity.

Perhaps Iffley's purchases were paid for out of public funds and eventually turned over to the funding authority. Treasure's further speculations on this line were short-lived: too short perhaps. The scenery was to engage both travellers for the remainder of the journey: immediately, a seascape had opened before them. 'My word, that's a powerful sight,' said the banker, and he meant it.

The road plunged down to Newgale Sands, ran beside the beach, then twisted and turned to higher ground where it remained elevated for some time until it made a mighty genuflection to pass through Solva—a village similar to Panty, but smaller and not so overdeveloped.

Two miles onwards and the little car was making one of its big-hearted charges up the Panty High Street.

'Turn right off the main road at the top . . . pass the church and vicarage on the right . . . big gates on the left before the road becomes a farm track.' Having manoeuvered the car according to the directions he was reciting, the Inspector drove it between the tall iron gates on to the wide gravelled drive that encompassed a perfect circle of lawn. 'That copper in Whitland really knew the way, sir.'

It seemed the car had scarcely come to rest before its driver had alighted and deposited Treasure's possessions beside the pointed porch.

I won't wait if you don't mind.' Iffley was clambering back into the car as Treasure was closing the nearside door. 'Judges make me nervous.' The car engine was already throbbing for the off. The policeman leant over to wave through the open passenger window. 'Glad to have been of service. Take care, sir.'

The departure was unceremonious in the extreme: perhaps judges made Inspector Iffley feel underdressed. Treasure found an iron bell-pull: it was well fashioned and in splendid working order. In answer to a tug, tollings seemed to echo from every quarter.

Not fifty yards from where Treasure now stood waiting, but beyond the tall gates, across the road and behind the low, vicarage wall, there crouched two small, excited figures and a large uninterested dog. The animal, an Irish wolf-hound, was not crouching to order but lying down because it was tired.

'It's him,' said Emma Wodd, the Vicar's daughter, aged nine, nearly.

'It's him all right.' Nye Evans—eight and a bit—nodded agreement. 'What do we do, Emma?'

Devalera (he's the dog) began to stretch in readiness for standing up. Emma and Nye threw themselves upon him for fear he should do anything so incautious.

CHAPTER 6

The clergyman had left Whitland Station unnoticed by anyone who mattered. He had recovered quickly—not quickly enough to have saved Treasure's involvement, but that had happened so soon after the attack as to have been unavoidable. He had been scarcely conscious, and certainly too dazed to use his quick wits. If it had not been for his invention and resource, he would hardly have gotten to Britain; first class all the way. You had to remember things like that, regularly fortifying yourself with positive thoughts when adversity struck.

He tended to lead a life where adversity threatened to strike often if left to its own devices. Positive thinking was a present help in any kind of trouble: it was what had got him down that corridor and into that washroom with the door locked behind him before anyone came looking.

By the time the train had backed up to Whitland he had been mentally composed and physically presentable. His face was washed and the skin abrasions on the forehead were dry enough. The wig could have been arranged to cover the powder burns, but he had decided to pocket it along with the moustache. Those goons had left his Burberry (after checking the pockets), and with this buttoned to the neck and with his crew-cut hair and dark glasses he would hardly have been recognized as the clergyman who boarded at Paddington.

His attackers had left him his wallet and most everything else on his person while they searched for the only thing they were after: his passport. They wouldn't take his word for it he didn't have the passport with him—even when with the gun at his head he was about to tell them the truth: that had been just before the thing went off, probably by mistake.

The noise of that explosion would go with him to the grave: the force of it had temporarily laid him out so that he could only surmise about what happened next. Chances were those punks had panicked, thinking they had somehow killed him with a blank cartridge: he'd felt dead and probably looked it. They must have grabbed his case and the parcel Treasure had left, hoping the passport was in one of them but with no time left to find out before they had to quit the train. It all fitted — and they surely needed that passport.

He had crossed the footbridge, walked through the booking office, the station forecourt and on to the main street without restraint or hesitation. It would have paid him to hesitate, to have mingled with the crowd and discovered the villains had failed to make off with their booty — notably his suitcase. He was not to learn this until later and well past the time when he might have risked reassuming his former appearance in order to claim his belongings. As it was, he had determined to get shot of Whitland as well as close contact with policemen.

He had caught a local bus to Haverfordwest. There he had bought a cheap but presentable overnight bag at one store and filled it with immediate requirements at two others — a chemist and a men's outfitters. He noticed the third shop sold clerical collars but he had not risked replacing the damaged one hidden by the raincoat: it would have made the sales assistant remember him that much better. In any case there was no purpose now in resurrecting that disguise.

The few phrases he had uttered during the transactions he had been careful to deliver in his nearly perfect English accent.

The last thing he bought was a stout walking stick with a heavy rubber tip. He did not intend to do any walking: you could protect yourself with a stick.

The bus had been the least conspicuous way of leaving Whitland, but he had made the journey from Haverford-west to St David's by taxi, keeping his raincoat done up to the neck.

The taxi-driver, known locally as Castrol Lloyd, would recall more than any counter clerk. He had sized up his passenger as well-built, and athletic with it, mid-thirties, probably foreign judging by the haircut, walked in to a door recently from the look of his forehead.

Castrol was well up on the variety of local subjects that entranced visitors. He failed to find one that produced more than a monosyllabic response during the whole of a fifteen-mile drive. The man had asked briefly about Panty as they had driven through — about how far it was from St David's: that was all.

The driver had his little victory in the end. 'Drop me in the middle of St David's' his passenger had ordered abruptly.

'This is the middle. Smallest cathedral city in Britain. Population 1,700. This is the square and that's the famous stepped Cross.' Visitors quickly came to think of the place as a village. 'The magnificent cathedral is in a dip over by there —'

"Let me out here. How much, and where's the Post Office?'

'You wouldn't want a hotel, like?' Castrol Lloyd's married sister worked in one. There was no question of commission: just a helpful word. But the passenger did not require anything more than directions to the Post Office which they had passed fifty yards back.

Some days later it was to go hard with Castrol that he was quite unable to add anything to the information on his fare other than what is set out here.

For his part, the cleric was well pleased with his progress. You could hardly say it had been uneventful, but he was here in St David's at 3.30, exactly the time he had aimed to arrive.

He had travelled with the very person he had been warned to avoid at all costs. He had been assaulted and robbed—he didn't think because of Treasure although it could have been Treasure who had fingered him without meaning to.

He had lost his passport along with everything else in his bag: that was a set-back but one that could be overcome. He was not likely to be recognized by Treasure and now that he knew the man, he could surely manage to avoid him for the hours he intended to be in the area. If the police were looking for him, they would only have Treasure's description to work with.

He had not expected to be set upon—and by amateurs. So, they had got the passport, but if they were also supposed to put the frighteners on him they had missed by a mile. The whole episode had been tawdry, risky for all concerned, and had made him even more determined to get the money. Now he was on his guard and would trust nobody. The idea of being civilized about this whole thing had been a blind from the beginning: he could see that now. Yet still he found it hard to believe that people who had been so close . . .

'I'm here like I said I'd be here.' He was speaking from the 'phone-box outside the little Post Office. 'I'm disappointed in you, but we'll let that pass. Let's just say my price is now the whole hundred grand plus the return of my passport.' There was an intake of breath at the other end of the line, but he was not waiting for words. 'I'll call back in an hour with a time and a place—a public place. You be ready, and remember who has the most to lose.'

Some distance back along the road into West Wales, Edgar J. Crabthorne and Patience, his bride for thirty-two wonderful years, were observing the passing scene without enthusiasm from the rear seats of a hired Daimler limousine.

There is a stretch of the Motorway skirting Swansea and Llanelli where the landscapers have given up hope of improving the vile industrial outlook on all sides and left it to the engineers to maintain the smoothest and safest possible road surface. Motorists thus proceed in comfort and at speed buoyed by the knowledge that some of the most ravishingly beautiful sea- and landscapes lie directly ahead. If they happen to be turning off for Swansea or Llanelli, then of course different kinds of compensations apply — probably to do with making money.

The chauffeur of the limousine, name of Ernest Grouch, appeared unmoved by aesthetic gloom and unaware of pending joys that would pend less if he drove faster. Unlike Castrol Lloyd, he spoke only when spoken to: in any case he was insulated from his passengers by an electrically controlled glass screen which for some reason was operating only from the switch next to the driver. This had involved Crabthorne in several times having to clamber across the intervening space to rap on the glass, indicate to Grouch that this should be lowered to allow for the issuing of orders, to make the necessary pronouncements, and then to clamber back again, each time forgetting to stipulate that the screen should be left in the lowered position.

'This man's a fool,' the President of the Hutstacker Chemical Corporation confided to his wife. 'Hasn't he ever heard of a bathroom? And I told him way back to move faster *and* leave that glass down. I simply said we needed to use the bathroom. He said there'd be one in the hotel. That's seventy miles from here. At the speed he's driving . . . Hell, we should have taken the train.'

'We were too late for the train, Edgar, and anyway, dear, you never liked trains.' It wasn't Mrs Crabthorne who needed the bathroom. An American matron of sound upbringing, she deplored circumlocution. 'Tell him to stop at the next gas station that has a john.'

'Crutt said a car would look more as though we were on vacation. It'll be handy if I need to run over to the plant, too.' The American's tone was grudging.

'Edgar, we *are* on vacation and you've seen the plant. You saw it months ago and you weren't impressed. In any case, Mr Crutt said it would be closed from lunch-time today until Tuesday.'

'And that's another thing. They take too many national holidays in this country.'

'Not as many as we do, dear.'

'And they strike too often.'

Patience Crabthorne gave an understanding smile. 'I expect they have their reasons.'

Crabthorne sometimes suspected Communist tendencies lurked behind that impeccable Daughter of the American Revolution façade. 'Maybe I should have tried harder to reach Treasure. He may be offended.'

Ten days had gone by since Lord Grenwood's luncheon-party at the Perceval Club, time for Crabthorne to have completed his fast, fact-finding tour of Hutstacker European offices and factories. His wife had not accompanied him beyond London, having no taste for one-night stops in Milan, Lyons, Rotterdam, Frankfurt and Helsinki.

Patience Crabthorne's notion of civilized travel had to do with steamships, Pullman coaches, large, tastefully furnished apartments, especially in Venice, and the absence of haste—all due less to experience than to a lifelong regard for the works of Henry James. She had been compromising with a riverside suite at the Savoy Hotel and a series of fresh visits to those cathedrals, fine houses, and picture galleries that lay within a day's march or ride of that estimable establishment. She was now looking forward to a week of discovery further afield and accompanied by her husband.

The spring trip to Europe was a regular event in the

Crabthorne calendar. On balance, Edgar gained less new information about his business than Patience gathered deepening understanding of Vanbrugh façades and Van Dyck portraits, but each drew satisfactions from their experiences.

Patience had been planning a round trip to Chester and York, but a telephone call late the night before from an agitated Albert Crutt had prompted Crabthorne to forswear pleasure and personally intervene in the matter of Judge Nott-Herbert and Rigley's Footbalm. He had been unable to reach Treasure that morning, but had learned the banker was actually en route for Wales. This was something of an embarrassment, since the American hesitated to begin his intervention without counselling with his adviser, even though time was short. It was his wife who had provided the tactful solution. The cathedral at St David's sounded quite as enthralling as the ones at Chester or York and provided ample reason innocently for Crabthorne to find himself within close calling distance of the Judge.

'Mark Treasure won't be in the least offended. It was Molly his wife who told me we ought to take in Wales at this time of year.' Patience Crabthorne was reinforcing her point.

'Crutt was pretty firm the Judge needed the kind of reassurances only I could give him.' Crabthorne paused. 'Personally.' He needed no convincing about his capacity to make a blurred situation crystal clear: Crutt had been counting on this.

'Say, there's a gas station, *and* it's advertising toilets. Edgar, tell Grouch to stop the car.' Crabthorne sighed and began to clamber forward.

'Thank God you've called. He's here. He rang me from a call-box. He's very angry.' The voice was agitated. 'He was attacked and robbed on the train. I think also hurt.

Did you arrange—'

'Just relax. Everything's under control.'

'But he's calling back later. He wants the whole hundred thousand and he won't come here. Says he'll name a place and—'

'Relax. You're not listening. There's been a bit of a foul-up, that's all. But I can straighten it out.'

'He says he wants his passport back. Who took his passport?'

'Whoever took it, pretty soon he's going to learn the police got it. Then we'll see who's calling the tricks.'

'The police have it! But that's worse . . .'

'I told you I can straighten it out but you have to trust me. Now just take some deep breaths or something.' The caller chuckled. 'When he rings again, make sure he knows the police got his baggage.'

'From the train? I don't understand. You said you'd see him on the train—reason with him. Thank God I told him to avoid this Treasure. They must have been on the same train.'

'Actually they travelled together.'

'Oh no! So now they know each other?'

'No—not really. It's complicated. Just do as I say. Tell him the police got his bag, but say we can get the passport back without him being involved. He'll go for that.'

'He won't believe me.'

'OK, tell him—tell him we've got his passport already and he can have it along with the hundred thou—'

'You were mad to think—'

'The whole hundred thou. No bargaining.'

'That's better.'

'He knows the let's-stay-friends bit was a sham.'

'Because you've had him mugged or something.'

'I don't want to go into that now, but he started it by upping the ante in the first place.'

'Justifiably.'

'I just thought some re-negotiating with the passport back on our side . . .'

'Where is it?'

'OK. Listen carefully. You have to move quickly . . .'

CHAPTER 7

New Hall, Panty, home of Judge Henry Nott-Herbert, had been fashioned in the style Mark Treasure—without hesitation or disparagement—dubbed Milwaukee Gothic: phoney but functional.

A confident residence of moderate size for a gentleman of better than moderate means, the banker dated it no earlier than the turn of the century. Central heating and basically sound plumbing would almost certainly have been original features and, with any luck, private bathrooms and water-closets for favoured guests.

The design, in stone, was two-storied with a dormered, battlemented attic. The northern façade presented pairs of mullioned bays rising through both floors on either side of the crenellated porch. The entrance was graceful—drop-arched, marble-shafted, and hung with half-glazed screen doors: the visible white-washed interior was fan-vaulted: the oak, pointed door to the main hall beyond stood open.

The whole edifice though created with integrity and taste lacked sympathy and originality. The architect could have been George Gilbert Scott—but hurriedly, on the back of a handy envelope. Wrong, Treasure mused, it was too late for Scott even though he was employed at St David's. One of the sons, perhaps . . . ?

'My dear Treasure. My apologies. Er . . . it is Mr Treasure? Nnn . . . Nott-Herbert is my name.'

The banker nodded confusedly. He had been too involved with his favourite sort of postulation, his gaze elsewhere, to have noticed his host's sudden appearance in the porch.

The Judge had thrown open the screen doors and made

a theatrical advance to the threshold. Of middle height, he was a standfast, upright figure evidently and determinedly defying wear-and-tear arthritis in the upper neck joints: head movements tended to stem from chest level.

The elegant double-breasted tweed suit was as much out of style as out of season: a flamboyant silk handkerchief blossomed from the topmost pocket. The voice was earnest and concerned: there had been nervous hesitancy only in the opening phrases. The facial expression was all eager anticipation. Fine hands reached out in welcome. Then, as Treasure began his audible response to the greeting, the expression changed dramatically.

The Judge's gaze moved sharply to the right, fixing in the middle distance over Treasure's shoulder. 'Bless my soul. Did you hear that?'

The banker turned. There was a group of outhouses to the east. Nott-Herbert now had one arm outstretched pointing at what looked like a garage door. The other hand half covered his mouth.

'Help! Help! Save me! I'm being kidnapped. In the garage.'

The voice was a convincing soprano and lacked nothing in urgency and drama. The weakness was that it evidently did not emanate from the garage but from the throat of Judge Nott-Herbert. Treasure found himself momentarily at a loss. Clearly he was in the presence of an amiable lunatic. Already the Judge had started in the direction of the garage. Should Treasure indulge the idiotic whim by going with him or else seek out whichever familiar acted as keeper—assuming there was such a person.

As Treasure stood irresolute, the Judge halted, turned about and let out a great sigh. 'Didn't work, did it?' The shoulders drooped forlornly, the hands dipped into the ample side pockets of the jacket. 'Weren't taken in for a second, were you? D'you see, I haven't got the knack of it at all.'

'I'm so sorry, I don't quite . . . ?'

'Ventriloquism, my dear fellow.' The Judge was now regarding the doll, where Treasure had placed it, but in a detached kind of way. 'Would you say I failed on projection or on illusion? Professor Popov is very strong on the importance of illusion. He wrote the instruction book. Don't suppose he's a Professor really.'

'No, I don't suppose so either.' Treasure was considerably relieved. 'I've brought the doll,' he added with a touch of apology.

'The dummy.'

'I'm sorry?'

'The Professor is very strong on nomenclature. It's a dummy. Remind you of anybody?'

'Stan Laurel.'

'Who?'

'The Laurel of Laurel and Hardy. Isn't that who it's supposed . . .'

'Yes, yes, I believe so. How very kind of you to have brought him. Have any trouble getting here?' The question was rhetorical, suggesting that so simple an expedition could hardly have presented obstacles. 'Davenport's, they're the people who make them up—dashed clever—said they'd deliver to the train. Rang them, you see. Said it was urgent. Very accommodating.'

The Judge was absently stroking the few silky strands of white hair that springing from around his left ear traversed the broad, balded pate—a credit to careful husbandry and effecting a coifed illusion that even Professor Popov might have considered laudable.

'Curious they didn't pack the thing more thoroughly.' Nott-Herbert was now considering the dummy close to. 'Must have been something of an embarrassment to you.'

'Not at all,' Treasure replied lightly, continuing with

equal lack of accuracy, 'The original packing was better, but we did have a slight accident on the way. I think you'll find Stanley the Dummy and adjuncts intact.'

'Most kind of you.' The reference to the accident seemed not to have registered. 'Well, come in. Come in. Tea will be ready soon outside in the garden.'

The Judge had tucked dummy and box under one arm without ceremony and, grasping Treasure's case with his free hand, was thrusting through the porch and into the hall. Impervious to well-mannered protest from his following guest, he placed both encumbrances on a broad untidy table.

'Welcome to my humble abode. Interested in architecture, are you? Of course you are. Clarence told me as much.' The Judge paused and looked about him leaving Treasure to identify the Clarence of mutual acquaintance. '1896. John Oldrid Scott, Gilbert Scott's younger son, not the one who went potty. Built it for my grandfather. Now he *was* potty, but he liked his comforts.'

'A keen organist?' The hall was impressive in its size and trappings—marble floor, angled stone staircase, wide upper gallery, pictures everywhere. What most impressed however, was the three-manual pipe organ against the rear wall. Treasure was gratified at having guessed the provenance of the building so nearly accurately. He wondered now whether to add the suggestion that Andrew Carnegie might have been a frequent and grateful guest.

'No. no. The organ's mine. Bought it three years ago. Came from an abandoned nonconformist chapel. Otherwise it was going for scrap. Shame.' The Judge contemplated his acquisition with pride. 'D'you play?'

'I'm afraid not . . .'

'Neither do I. Thought I'd take it up sometime. Haven't got round to it yet, though. Applied to join the Magic Circle.'

The last fact was clearly intended to offer the definitive reason why the speaker had put aside competing ambitions. If the voice-throwing performance earlier was typical of the standard of magic and illusion so far achieved, Treasure considered it might be less fanciful of the Judge to concentrate on a musical career.

'Remind me to show you a trick or two. Ah!' Nott-Herbert had swivelled ninety degrees to greet a breathless and red-faced, well-upholstered matron. Short, grey-haired but still comely, she had virtually blown in, the green baize door still flapping in her wake. 'And this is Mrs Evans, Mrs Blanche Evans my estimable housekeeper, from whom all . . . er . . . all pleasures flow . . . er . . . yes.'

The Judge and the object of his flowery misquotation appeared mutually satisfied with the aptness of the introduction.

Mrs Evans was enveloped in a starched white overall of ankle length, hands clasped prayerfully and resting on her ample, heaving middle. Her costume, joyous countenance and invocative posture suggested a winded acolyte gathering strength for a loud Amen.

'Came quick as I could.' The voice was indeed musical, as was the native cadence. 'Nye, that's my little grandson, saw you arrive, but I was down the garden. Oh, it is so good to see you, Mr Treasure. His Honour's come up trumps as per usual.' She glanced approvingly at her employer. 'The Bishop said you'd help, too.'

'I'm delighted to meet you.' Treasure offered his hand. He was charmed if a little surprised at the evident warmth of the greeting. He was also certain he was not acquainted with the Bishop of St David's: he had checked in Crockford's Clerical Directory the night before.

Mrs Evans gave a little bob as they shook hands. 'And lovely manners too.' she offered disarmingly. 'Wait till Ethel Ogmore-Davies meets him.' This was added in a knowing sort of aside to the Judge.

'Yes, well, if you'd show Mr Treasure to his room . . .'
Nott-Herbert was obviously as uneasy as his guest was
baffled by some of the housekeeper's outpouring.

'This way then, sir. There's thoughtless I am. Dying for
a cup of tea you'll be and wanting to wash up first.'

Mrs Evans, pausing only to throw an enigmatic grimace
at 'Stan Laurel', had firmly grasped Treasure's bag and
was halfway up the first flight of stairs while still engaged
on these newest observations. Already she was breathing
heavily again, partly from the pace at which she moved
and partly because she attacked each stone step as though
it were several inches higher than it actually was.

'Let me take the bag.'

'Not a bit. Tired you'll be after that nasty old journey.'
Mrs Evans, straight-backed if listing slightly bagwards,
was continuing her high stepping progress ahead. 'Came
by train and taxi I expect, did you?' Then, without
waiting for confirmation. 'Quicker than car, they say,
even with the new road. The Bishop and his wife came
last month in their Mini. Took ever such a long time.
From near Oxford,' she added with a sort of reverence.

'From Mitchell Stoke?'

'That's right, and this is your room, sir.'

So it was *that* Clarence, Bishop Clarence Wringle,
another retired Colonial, who had been proffering information on Treasure's interests to the Judge as well as the
banker's predisposition to help as relayed by Mrs Evans.
For the first time Treasure wondered whether his
presence in Panty had been altogether occasioned by his
involvement with the Hutstacker Chemical Corporation.
The last time he had been closely concerned with the
diminutive Bishop the subject had been neither religious
nor commercial: it had been murder.[1]

[1] For details see *Unholy Writ*

'Lemon or milk? They're both there. Help yourself, my dear chap.' The Judge and Treasure were seated opposite each other at a tea-table prepared for three on the sheltered, south terrace. 'Room all right? Everything you want up there? If not tell Mrs Evans. Whatever it is, she'll have it. Marvellous woman. Marvellous.' Nott-Herbert returned his full attention to something he was arranging below table height.

The apartment provided for Treasure was elegant by any standard. The exquisite furnishings in both the bedroom and dressing-room he approved as warmly as he did the totally up to date arrangements in the carpeted bathroom. He too liked his comforts, and whatever the true reason for the summons to Panty, he was already regretting that the stay was scheduled to be short—also that his wife had not come with him.

He had taken longer than had been strictly necessary before joining his host. After concluding that the signed Vuillard lithograph over the fireplace in the bedroom and the small Utrillo painting beside the tallboy in the dressing-room were exactly what they appeared to be, it had been necessary as a penance for vulgar doubting to stop to admire them properly.

'The arrangements are delightful and—'

'And surprisingly civilized,' the Judge interrupted, looking up with a wry smile. 'One may live in the back of beyond but that's no reason . . . Got it. Watch this.' His right hand appeared first from beneath the table, a golfball clasped between thumb and first finger. The Judge extended his whole right arm upwards. 'See. Nothing up my sleeve.'

That there was evidently nothing up the Judge's right sleeve served only to accentuate that there was almost certainly something up the left one. His next move was to tug at his right sleeve to prove its innocence with a left hand conjoined to an arm that appeared in some way to have shrivelled or become deformed. It was obviously key that the left elbow should remain tightly crooked while the tugging was going on—an effect that the Judge was sadly unable to sustain.

A trickle of golf-balls emerged from the general area of the Judge's inside upper left arm. They cascaded on to the stone-flagged terrace bouncing in all directions and by their behaviour declaring that they were simulated golf-balls made of celluloid. The last fact was confirmed by the action of an immense Irish wolfhound recently arrived on the scene.

Devalera was not concerned to chase the balls: any that came close enough to where he was standing to be arrested without effort he stamped on, flattened with a huge front paw and ate.

'Damn!' the Judge exploded. 'That trick is far from perfect.'

Treasure was hastily retrieving the errant balls that had escaped the notice or reach of the dog, which had now lowered itself in to a sitting position. 'That animal looks as though he's come out without his saddle,' the banker observed brightly. He placed the recaptured balls in the empty slop basin.

'It's really a very simple trick,' said the Judge, ignoring the dog. 'It's called the multiplying ball trick.' He looked from the slop basin to the object in his right hand which had now become two objects—one simulated golf-ball, and half a simulated golf-ball, the latter having earlier fitted over part of the former. 'Of course it's easier if you don't use so many balls. This half one looks like a whole ball if you handle it well.' The Judge promptly dropped it in his tea.

There followed a few moments of embarrassed silence, then the Judge observed ruminatively. 'Tomorrow I'll just stick to my ventriloquist performance. Should go down well with the children. The new dummy ought to be quite a draw.' He glanced without too much confidence at the object in question which was now lying, still boxed, on an empty chair beside him.

'What's happening tomorrow?' Treasure was sipping his tea vaguely conscious that he should somehow be bringing the conversation round to the purpose of his visit.

'Annual opening of the garden to every Tom, Dick and Harry in aid of the Lifeboats. Nothing much to see for 50p really.' Nott-Herbert gestured across the lawn.

Treasure had, on the contrary, been impressed by both the size and attractiveness of the big walled garden first viewed from his bedroom and now at closer quarters. On ground falling seawards the two or so cultivated acres were protected from the north by the house and in other aspects by judiciously placed, matured trees and hedging. Heather beds were islanded in the lawn which was thickly bordered by flowering shrubs. Below the terrace well-kept rose-beds were beginning to show colour. This most formal part of the garden was dissected by wide paved walks.

'I think it charming and well worth the money.'

'There's tea as well, bunfight here on the terrace. That's another 75p. Usually we have a Punch and Judy for the children but he's left the area. Thought I'd stand in. Been practising.' The Judge looked doubtful. 'No charge for that, of course,' he added defensively.

'Very sporting of you, and in a good cause. Anyway it sounds as though you have a busy time ahead. I wonder when we might touch on this Hutstacker business?'

'The what?'

'The question of Hutstacker Chemical buying Rigley & Herbert.' Treasure gave a smile. 'The reason I came down.'

'Oh, that. Do whatever you like, my dear chap. Clarence was absolutely confident in your judgement as well as in the more important matter . . . Bit of luck the old boy was here . . . knowing you and all that. We were exact contemporaries at the University. "Get Treasure down here", he said to me. "Straighten you out in no time". And here you are.' The Judge looked eminently pleased and ready to be straightened out.

'Very good of Clarence to say so, but I *am* advising Hutstacker's.' Treasure felt it incumbent he should make the point.

'Americans.' Nott-Herbert wrinkled his nose. 'All right, are they? Not had much to do with Americans.' He looked up. 'Produced some great jurists, of course.'

'These are first-rate people. I think they want to develop the business, and the price is . . . er . . . quite attractive, not to say generous.' Though whether this would matter to a man who hung original Neo-Impressionists in his guest rooms, Treasure could only conjecture.

'To be sure. I was against it at the start, you know.' Treasure hadn't known. The Judge seemed momentarily disarmed. 'It's your view I should sell. It's also the view of the lady to whom I am . . . er . . . the widow lady who has consented to become my wife—and bless my soul, here she is, absolutely on cue.'

The dog had already stirred itself and was advancing amiably, gaze fixed in the same direction as the Judge's, which was over Treasure's shoulder.

The banker turned and began to rise, expecting to greet a lady of mature years, younger perhaps than the widower Judge, for that was usually the way of things, but a seemly consort in old age.

A moment later Treasure found himself facing a breathtakingly, even thrillingly beautiful young woman.

CHAPTER 8

The trouble with beautiful women is that, like Everest, they are there, thought Treasure.

In the ten minutes since Anna Spring had first appeared he had been attempting, without any marked success, to regard her objectively and dispassionately as the future Mrs Nott-Herbert: he recognized that the mental challenge was more to do with mild envy than plain incredulity—and that both instincts were unworthy.

Here was a truly delicious woman—tall, slim, boyish figure; long, nearly blonde hair; exquisitely chiselled features; big, searching blue eyes and a mouth that was just gently provocative. She moved like a dancer: her voice was soft and husky—the accent German-American, the English phraseology at times charmingly pedantic.

Her clothes were simple and casual—a silk shirt, jeans, sandals, a cashmere cardigan draped across the shoulders: simple, casual and expensive.

'You believe it can be left in this way, Mr Treasure, so . . . so inconclusive?' The tone indicated real concern. The expressive hands cupped the exquisite chin, levelling and steadying the gaze in the banker's direction.

'Certainly not,' said Treasure, against his better judgement, 'and, please, do call me Mark.' He defied Molly, his wife, to classify this exceptional creature as common.

'But the police have lost interest already. Very un-British, I think.' She smiled.

'Not these days, I'm afraid. They're understaffed and the crime rate is rising.' He was being worldly, not pompous.

'This follows, of course.'

'I think you're probably right, though it's not . . .'

'Not axiomatic, you'd say. Is that correct?'

'Perfectly.' It was of course axiomatic that Molly considered all women he found as attractive as Anna to be common: even the ones with inherited titles.

'And you're ready to do a bit of sleuthing.' The Judge beamed. 'My dear chap, I can't tell you how grateful we'll be.'

'Mrs Ogmore-Davies is so very sweet.' This was Anna. 'And she is very upset. She is believing that people think her stupid which she is not. She was so kind to me when I came back. When it was difficult for me.'

'Quite so, my dear. I'm sure Mark will do all he can.' Nott-Herbert glanced benignly at his guest. 'Local constable's a decent sort of chap, by the way, just ineffective. Wife's a harridan. Left him twice. Back now I think— more's the pity. Got his own cross to bear. Even so he should have taken the whole business further at the time. Couldn't be bothered.'

'The police took the view that Mrs . . . er . . . what's her name . . . Mrs Ogmore-Davies was mistaken in what she saw—or thought she saw?' Why was he going along with the notion, he wondered, that he was some kind of latter-day Sexton Blake? He should have been protesting that the Judge had fetched him to West Wales under entirely false pretences—on the suggestion of a meddling old prelate. 'And there were no other witnesses—or possible witnesses?' It would be churlish, perhaps, not to hum for his supper at least. And the Hutstacker business seemed to be wrapped up.

'See. I told you so.' The Judge was triumphant. 'Mark's got it in one. Did the police look for other witnesses? People who wouldn't come forward unless pressed? I'll wager they didn't.'

'They may have done,' Treasure offered cautiously.

'They didn't ask me.' Anna looked from Treasure to the Judge. And then she looked back again. 'I could have been strolling along the harbour, at six in the morning, in the rain, and happened to see a naked man.' She smirked.

'I'll vouch you were doing nothing of the kind, my dear.' The Judge was mildly shocked, and curiously adamant.

'But if you had, you'd have said so. Two kinds of people wouldn't,' Treasure continued sagely. 'The guilty for one reason or another, and those not wanting to get involved, also for one reason or another. It wasn't that early in the morning, and I'd be surprised if Mrs Ogmore-Davies was the only possible witness to what she said she saw.' He paused. 'Anyway, tomorrow's a Saturday and I'll see for myself who the early birds are.'

'Bully for you, Mark. But Anna will tell you there's a lot more activity now in the harbour than there is at Easter, at all times of the day — and half the night.'

'It's also a lot lighter at six than it was two months ago. Would you like to meet Mrs Ogmore-Davies at five-thirty today?' Anna asked efficiently. He nodded. 'Then that's arranged.'

'I'd like to do that, and see the harbour — and this lovely garden, and the church opposite.'

Anna looked puzzled. 'But the garden and the church, they have nothing to do with —'

'With Mrs Ogmore-Davies's dead body. It happens I enjoy gardens and old churches. They'll be my reward.'

'And Anna, my dear, you shall be his guide because I have to rehearse for my performance tomorrow.' The Judge began to turn stiffly in his chair towards the so far neglected dummy. But Anna was quicker, springing from her seat to kneel beside the box.

'He is hardly — would you say — endearing?' She picked up the dummy gingerly: not like a baby. 'So you can have him,' she began, passing Stanley to the Judge, 'but may I have the box, Henry? I have a small business where packing materials cost a fortune.'

She had turned to make the last remark to Treasure and in doing so by accident knocked the box with her arm. It slid off the chair and on to the ground where it was immediately pounced upon by Devalera. The dog was evidently used to being awarded such discards: this one seemed actually to have been aimed to drop at his feet.

The animal began cavorting around the lawn, the unwieldy box grasped firmly in his giant maw.

'Oh Henry, darling, stop him!'

'Devalera, you awful dog, sit. SIT!'

The dog's response was to stop in the centre of the lawn and to lower his *front* half to the ground. The box he firmly pinioned with his outstreched forelegs while his huge jaw began tearing away at its centre. Ferocious growling accompanied the demolition process while suspicious canine eyes glowered to left and right, watching for hostile approaches.

Devalera's tail meantime wagged contentedly at the elevated end of his monstrous being, where rear legs were braced for instant flight. Altogether, one box was worth any number of simulated golf-balls in an afternoon that had offered few enough distractions.

The Judge rose from his seat at the tea-table and strode purposefully towards the animal. 'Devalera, drop it. Stupid name for a dog. Stupid dog. Drop it, I say.'

As his master grew close the animal reared back on all fours, side-stepped the approach with booty still intact and bounced a few yards before adopting his former position and dissolute occupation.

Since Treasure had been at some pains earlier in the day to safeguard this box as well as its contents, and since Anna had declared a nobler future for it than destruction by Irish wolfhound, the banker stepped forward heroically.

'Here, dog,' he said, firmly brandishing a chocolate digestive biscuit. 'I'll have that, old boy.'

If Treasure had been marginally quicker grasping the

temporarily abandoned box or if Devalera had taken the decent interval usually required even by hungry dogs to consume a whole chocolate digestive biscuit, the contest between man and beast could have been over there and then. Unfortunately Devalera swallowed biscuits whole, and instead of walking away with the box Treasure found himself for the second time that day hanging on to one end of it while the gigantic dog gnarled and pulled at the other, delighted with the game.

This second tug-of-war was doomed to end quickly. Devalera had already nearly torn through the middle of the box and before even Treasure had time to give up the unequal struggle the thing parted in the centre.

'I'm so sorry,' the banker turned laughing towards Anna Spring, holding his piece of box while the dog strutted around head high trying to keep his half aloft. It was then that the small, flat object slid out of the wrappings and fell to the ground. Treasure picked it up.

'It's a passport,' he said to the others. 'Property of . . .' He studied the cover and then began to leaf through the front pages. 'Property of Mr D. E. Rees . . . Mr Dylan Emrys Rees, clerk by profession and born in Panty thirty-five years ago tomorrow.'

'Gemini,' the Judge announced loudly. 'Surprising number of old Panty people were born in June. Consequence of the warm Septembers we get here.'

The others were more interested in the passport than the commentary on local mating habits. 'Issued recently and so far unused for travel abroad. Either of you know him?' Treasure displayed the photograph of D. E. Rees to his two companions.

'It's not Dai Rees the postman. He was here today. Could have dropped it. But it's not him.' Nott-Herbert finished uncertainly. He gave Anna an enquiring glance.

'The first name is Dylan, and anyway it doesn't look a bit like the postman, Henry. But there are many other

Reeses.' Anna's tone was almost jaunty. 'We should perhaps give it to the police?'

'I just wonder how it got in that box. There's nothing else in my half except the remains of the tissue paper.'

'Nor in this.' The Judge had retrieved the other piece of the box now abandoned by Devalera in the fickle manner of dogs.

Treasure studied the photograph again. He had never understood why some people knowingly settled for passport photographs technically indifferent and personally insulting. His own was mildly flattering.

The photograph before him had been badly lit and offered a washed-out image of what seemed a half-witted subject. Conceivably the subject was a very pale half-wit. Alternatively, the poor definition and blank expression could both have been contrived.

Treasure considered the obvious—that the passport belonged to the vanished Australian cleric from the train. Someone in the habit of wearing disguise at least had a reason for avoiding good photographic likenesses of himself. The clergyman could have found a way of slipping the passport into the parcel and the face in the picture, decorated with wig and moustache, could just be Treasure's mysterious travelling companion.

The passport should be handed to the police as Anna had suggested. Treasure wondered whether it should be given to Detective-Inspector Iffley rather than the local constable described by the Judge as ineffective. He then recalled he had no way of making contact with Iffley. He had so far given no one in Panty an account of his adventure on the train: he balked at the notion of resurrecting the narrative for the local bobby and for the purpose of illustrating a probably bogus theory about a mislaid passport.

It was just that he could not credit how a parcel that

had been in his charge for most of the day had acquired a passport unless . . .

'On the hall table, Your Honour. It could have been there, brought in lost, like, and sort of been dropped into the box.' Mrs Blanche Evans had come to clear the tea things and had her own notion about where the passport had come from. 'Proper lost and found department we are, Mr Treasure. Some think we're the Vicarage, and Constable Lewin lives right down at the bottom of the hill, so people can't be bothered. Was it for signing, like? They do come to have their passports signed by His Honour. Cheek.'

'That would be for a passport application, Mrs Evans,' Treasure said, unravelling the various threads in the jumbled commentary. 'People might ask the Judge to sign the photos one has to send.'

'They get a flea in the ear if they do. Job for the Vicar,' Nott-Herbert declared stoutly. 'People do leave things on that table, though. And the children put anything delivered there. Could you ask Nye, Mrs Evans? Otherwise I'll telephone Lewin. Tell him we've got a lost passport.'

'No need, darling, I can give it him when we see him later.' Anna took the passport from Treasure, who abandoned it gladly along with the dilemma it had been presenting.

'As you wish, my dear, but perhaps I should take charge of it. And now I must rehearse.'

The Judge made towards the house, following in the wake of the tray-laden Mrs Evans. Half way he stopped and turned, the dummy now cradled in one arm. 'How's this?' he cried.

He took a further moment to compose his features. 'That's another fine mess you've got us into Stanley,' he offered in a voice just discernibly different from his normal tones but not remotely reminiscent of the late Oliver

Hardy. He then began to manipulate the head of the dummy but without much dexterity: it soon faced backwards to the body and appeared to stick in that position.

'Devilishly tricky,' Nott-Herbert observed almost to himself as he turned and continued towards the house.

He pulled the head from the dummy, an action that gave Mrs Evans, who observed it, quite a turn.

CHAPTER 9

'What you call a grand old British gentleman.' Anna's gaze followed the retreating figure of the man she was to marry. Then she looked directly at Treasure. 'I am not a scheming female taking advantage. I love him very deeply.' She hesitated. 'Like a daughter.' Then asked defiantly, 'is that wrong?'

Treasure admired the candour. 'It's none of my business, of course.' He smiled. 'No, I don't think it wrong. The marriage will be for love, but . . .'

'But for convenience also. It will be for spiritual and material reasons—not physical ones, I think.' She spoke the last words deliberately. 'Henry wants me to inherit his money.'

'Without paying boring death duties. How very sensible.' Inwardly Treasure debated how advanced into dotage he would need to be before settling for a solely spiritual relationship with Anna Spring. Perhaps the lady underestimated her regenerative powers—or else the Judge had decided discretion was the better path to survival. Aloud he continued affably, 'I hope Henry is immensely rich.'

'He's rich, and he's seventy-three. I am thirty-two. His wife died some years ago, his son and daughter-in-law too . . . in an accident. They had no children. There is no one otherwise, except little Nye, that's Mrs Evans's grandson. Henry thinks of him as family. He's such an endearing child. We both adore him.' She slipped her arm through his. 'Come, we can walk through the garden as you wanted before I take you to meet Mrs Ogmore-Davies.'

'I'm sorry to burden you like this.'

'No you're not, and in any case we find one another attractive. So.' She shrugged her shoulders. 'The church you can do on your own, and the harbour too, in the morning as you said. We have an hour only now. I have to change in time to dine with you and Henry before the recital.'

'What recital?'

'Didn't Henry tell you? In the cathedral. A local amateur organist who murders Bach. I have to be there, but if I were you I'd beg to be excused. You're fond of Bach?'

'Passionately.'

'So the Bishop told us. Your wife too?'

Treasure nodded. 'I'm sorry she's not here.' A relative truth since if she had been it was doubtful he would be strolling through a secluded garden arm in arm with an entrancing woman who had just announced she found him attractive. 'Your husband . . . ?' An enquiry of some kind seemed appropriate.

'My husband was killed in an air crash over a year ago.'

'I'm sorry.'

'We were very much in love. He ran a small air charter business out of Miami. He'd been a second pilot with the big airlines . . .'

'He was American?'

She nodded. 'I'd been a stewardess for a while. That's how we met. But Ralph wanted to run his own company—not work for anyone else. You understand?'

'Of course. And it worked out?'

'Until he was killed in a freak storm somewhere between Tampico and Miami. He needn't have been flying. He'd been delivering a plane to a Mexican buyer—just a ferrying job. He was to return next day on a scheduled flight but he ran into another charter pilot returning empty to Miami. He rang me to say he'd accepted a free ride home . . . to be with me. It was a single engine plane.

It just . . . just disappeared.' Her hand tightened on Treasure's arm.

'I think you'd rather not talk about it.'

'No, no. It's good that I can speak of it now. For a while I was crazy with grief—and guilt. I felt responsible for his death. I couldn't stay in America. Too many memories. I destroyed all the tangible ones. Even Ralph's pictures. Stupid.' She sighed. 'I went back to Germany—my home, my mother's home is in Hamburg. May we sit a moment?'

They had taken a wide path that led from the lawn through banks of tall flowering shrubs. There was a seat in an arbour of deep purple lilac and soft pink rhododendrons.

'What brought you to Panty?'

'I came first many years ago as an *au pair* to learn English.'

'And Welsh as well?' Treasure chuckled.

'Sure, that was a bonus.' She smiled. 'My father, he was in the merchant navy, knew Captain Ogmore-Davies. We were not rich. My father was not also a Captain, you understand. Mrs Ogmore-Davies needed help in the house, unofficially with a small wage.' She shrugged her shoulders. 'So it worked very well for me to come here.'

'And you did learn excellent English.'

'Some, yes. But mostly now it's Americanized.' She drew her legs up to the seat, clasped them at the ankles and rested her chin on her knees. 'I came here to recapture peace of mind. It's a very special place for me. Oh, I know it's now a little commercial, but only in the season.'

'You kept in touch with your friends here?'

'With the Ogmore-Davieses, some others, and with Henry, of course.'

'You knew the Judge when you were here before?'

She nodded, laughing. 'Then he was learning German. Always he has needed to learn new things. It was nearly ten years ago. His wife was still alive, she was an invalid.'

'And he hired you to teach him German.'

'Not very well, I'm afraid.' She had picked a lilac leaf and was studying its composition as she talked. 'But his wife liked me to come—and the indispensable Mrs Evans too. She was very close to the Ogmore-Davieses.'

'I suppose the community was much smaller in those days.'

'Mmm—I could never have opened an art gallery then.'

'Is that the business you spoke about?'

She looked up with a glint of pride. 'There was a little insurance money. I studied history of art in America and worked in a gallery there for a while. It seemed a good risk to take with so many tourists around.'

'Where is the gallery?'

'Half way down the hill. It's two converted cottages on the High Street. I live over the shop—it's very snug, with a glorious view of the harbour at the back. You must come . . .'

'To buy a picture or to see the view?' He was consciously if harmlessly flirting with this very uncommon woman— and aware he had been encouraged.

Devalera had now rejoined the pair and was lying at Anna's feet. It was difficult to discern from his permanent hang-dog expression whether the coloured object, part of which was protruding from his mouth, was any more to his taste than the remains of the box which he had now evidently abandoned. Treasure bent down to retrieve the morsel which the dog seemed content—even anxious—to deliver up. It was a playing card.

'Behold the Eight of Hearts, or what's left of it,' said Treasure holding up his prize.

'It's the Six of Spades on this side.' Anna giggled.

'Who'd believe we have an Irish wolfhound that does card tricks?' He smirked at Anna, adding, as he slipped the card into his pocket. 'And he seems to do them better than Henry.'

The heated indoor whirlpool at the Panty Sunfun Hotel is circular and measures twelve feet across.

This gave room enough for each of the three present occupants to enjoy 'the stimulating caress of the six hundred powered water jets that ease away tension and tone-up the body beautiful in just about any position.'

The Sunfun Hotel Corporation of America considered the heated indoor whirlpool 'available at all our locations' to be a major selling proposition. Most guests preferred a private shower to the prospect of mass stimulation, whatever the position.

Indeed, most guests preferred a Hilton or a Holiday Inn if there was one available. Panty offered no such alternative.

Panty was able to offer a Sunfun Hotel because the Welsh Development Council had made a building subsidy on two other more commercially promising Sunfun locations dependent on the erection of a third at distant Panty. More accurately, the hotel sits on a cliff-top site overlooking a spectacular but inaccessible beach a mile beyond Panty on the way to St David's. At the time of the deal the Sunfun Hotel Corporation of America had shrugged its corporate shoulders, figured it was getting the third hotel for nothing, and put in an extra large whirlpool.

'I enjoy the whirlpool. Stay at a Sunfun whenever I can,' Edgar J. Crabthorne observed to the others: he had a sizeable private investment in Sunfun stock. 'Marvellous exercise,' he added, but this time more in the direction of Mrs Bronwen Crutt whose gyrating contours were providing stimulation as advertised.

While Crabthorne and Crutt were content to sit chest deep on the underwater step at the pool edge, Mrs Crutt had abandoned herself to the 'free-floating, cross-current massage' available at the centre of the whirlpool.

Bronwen was the second Mrs Crutt. The first one had demanded a divorce after twenty-two years of sheer boredom. Bronwen lacked the wit to be bored, was a good listener, and seldom spoke: she was a better wife to Albert Crutt than ever she had been a secretary. This was a relative comparison since she had never really mastered shorthand, but was sound enough on supplying the primeval satisfactions to a spouse who enjoyed doing the cooking himself. She was a handsome brunette built on generous curves, all of which could be viewed to advantage as she swooped, twisted and wiggled in the turbulent water.

Crabthorne considered the possibility that the fastenings on the brief bikini would fail to withstand the strain. From experience he knew such mischance was remote but not without precedent: another reason he preferred staying in Sunfun Hotels.

'Great idea of yours to book us all in here for the weekend, Arthur,' he observed amiably to Albert Crutt, but without removing his gaze from the Amazonian Bronwen. He edged along the submerged seat towards Crutt the better to exchange confidences, although the three had the whirlpool dome entirely to themselves. 'So you figure Treasure won't be strong enough to tip the Judge in our favour after all, Arthur.'

'It's Albert.'

'Where?' Crabthorne looked around hastily.

'I'm Albert. It doesn't matter.' The self-effacing Crutt had earlier been convinced that even the Governor of the Bank of England could not have persuaded Nott-Herbert to sell out to Americans. It was only when he had learned about the intervention of Mrs Anna Spring a few days before that he had begun to see his world crumble about him. Crabthorne was his only hope. 'You're our only hope, Edgar,' he continued sincerely.

'Nice of you to feel that way, Art—I mean Al. But you don't think I have to up the ante?'

'I don't think so. The Judge is quite rich. You need to emphasize your plans for expansion—in England. You mentioned you intended moving the factory to London . . .'

'Folding it into the Hutstacker plant at Ealing, sure. Rationalization is all these days. But Rigley & Herbert will survive in more than name . . .'

'In Ealing. The Judge will like to know that.'

'You don't think it'll be tactless to rub in we'll be closing down the Llanelli plant?' Considering Bronwen, which he was still doing intently, perhaps he could find a slot for Crutt in the new set-up after all: he liked his lady friends to be married to men who depended on him.

'Phasing the Welsh work out gradually, I think you said.' Crutt didn't want the Judge to miss any of the phraseology.

'With jobs for all the work staff who want to re-locate. You see, Al, we at Hutstacker really care about our people.' He could certainly care for Bronwen. 'Why, in the last decade . . .'

'Don't forget about the new packaging.' Every jar of Rigley's Footbalm had carried the effigy of a great-grandfather of the Judge's—distaff but venerated—since the product had first been produced in 1908. Nott-Herbert would need to know that was to be changed.

In fact Crutt had only needed to recite this list of heresies to the Judge four weeks earlier to have the older man dismiss with contempt any possibility of his parting with effective ownership of the family firm.

The Judge had been on the brink of empowering Crutt to relay his decision to Hutstacker's. But for Mrs Ogmore-Davies and her wretched dead body the Americans would have been sent packing long since. The invitation to Treasure had not represented a change of heart, only an intended short delay.

Since the Judge had now so firmly had his mind altered for him, it was absolutely necessary for him to be exposed to this preposterous commercial rapist—a term more apposite than Crutt divined—who gave nothing for tradition or loyalty, and who seriously imagined the good Welsh people of Llanelli would be ready to 're-locate' in suburban London. Not that Crutt, who was vaguely Anglo-Scottish, cared a damn for the perishing Welsh, with the exception of Bronwen: he cared a good deal about his job and the unlikelihood of his getting another if the Machiavellian Crabthorne turned him out at fifty-two.

'What time did you say we were due at the Judge's?' The American, planning to tangle awhile in the cross-currents, had already cast off for the centre of the whirlpool.

'At seven for drinks and probably dinner.' Crutt did not trouble to add that the arrangement had been made only an hour before, on the telephone, with the Judge's housekeeper, that Nott-Herbert had been engaged at the time and Treasure out visiting. He hoped most warmly that the practically unheralded arrival of four self-invited guests expecting dinner would cause their host the maximum irritation, and that Treasure would be equally vexed to learn that Crabthorne evidently did not trust him to cope here alone.

'That'll be fine, Art—Al, I mean—Ow!' The free-floating Crabthorne had just been kneed in the stomach by the cross-currenting Bronwen.

'Emma, my knees are hot. Why d'you think they're hot?' Nye, the grandson of Mrs Blanche Evans, carefully examined the offending members. 'Emma, d'you think it's because I'm early-germinated?'

'Illegitimate,' Emma Wodd corrected. ' 'Course not, silly.'

'Brenig Price at school says it *could* be because I'm illee . . . what you said, and his father drives an ambulance.'

'Well, that doesn't make him a real doctor, and anyway it's wrong. My knees get hot sometimes and I'm not illegitimate. It's the sun.' She stood up. 'I expect they've gone to Mrs Ogmore-Davies's.'

The two children had earlier been holding off a Zulu attack on their jungle hide-out, supplies nearly exhausted, when Anna and Treasure had settled on the seat close by.

'They said that's where they were going. Is there any Coke left?'

'No, it's all gone. We should have coughed or something.'

'Why? It wasn't secrets.' Nye had found the adult conversation boring. 'Devalera nearly gave us away.' He giggled. 'My Gran asked if someone left a posspot. What's a posspot? Sounds rude, like a p—'

' 'Tisn't,' the Vicar's daughter cut in, 'it's like a book.'

'Oh.' He tried licking his left knee and comparing the result with the right one. 'Mrs Ogmore-Davies told my Gran that Anna shouldn't marry the Judge.'

'Why not?'

'Because by rights my Gran should get the money.'

'What money?'

'I dunno. That's what she said.'

'P'raps that's why they're seeing Mrs Ogmore-Davies.'

'No it's not. My Gran says it's about the body, and Anna's being specially nice to Mrs Ogmore-Davies.'

'Because she doesn't want her to marry the Judge?'

'I dunno.' He looked a little bashful. 'I love Anna,' he said before licking his right knee and changing the subject. 'Shouldn't we have told him, Emma?'

'How could we have told *him*.'

Nye was closely comparing his knees. 'They're cooling

off, Emma. P'raps it was the Coke.' He looked up. 'Would you be punished much 'cos we were there?'

'Yes. Daddy said it was dangerous and should be knocked down and we weren't ever to climb up.'

'My Gran says he's a detective.' They made sense to each other.

'Can't be. Not a proper one. He's too posh.'

As an avid television viewer Nye had to agree. 'Can we play hospitals in your shed, Emma?'

'All right.' She scrambled to her feet. 'Race you there, but it's my turn to operate.'

They ran down the path to the garden gate and back along the road to the Vicarage. Devalera went along for the lollop, bounding with ease through dense and expensive shrubbery and emitting a deep slow bark that suggested a run-down battery.

CHAPTER 10

Treasure had the feeling that the dining-room at Mariner's Rest was seldom used for eating—or for anything else except possibly funeral wakes.

It was a dark room with a single window, lace-curtained against intrusive viewing from the lane outside. The furniture was highly polished, late Victorian Ugly supplemented by an unusual number of nondescript, un-matched chairs occupying most of the floor space including some that would have been better reserved for the movement of human beings.

Constable Lewin knew Mrs Ogmore-Davies conducted her 'meditation meetings' here—events reportedly attended by beings unhindered in their movements by a deficiency of anything so cosmic as floor space, or even floor boards. He found the aura of disembodied spirits intimidating, particularly as he did not believe in such things. He had arrived early—before the others—to imply he was keen, and had been lectured for his pains. He was present as a favour to Mrs Spring and out of deference to the Judge. He had been careful to show a proper respect to Treasure and to stop short of overtly humouring the old baggage who had kept the whole festering subject open—this in the hope of getting it closed once and for all.

Even without heavy oilskins Mrs Ogmore-Davies was a big woman, larger and older than her friend and re-mote relative Mrs Blanche Evans, and much less good-humoured.

'It isn't funny to be laughed at in your own village, Mr Treasure.' She stared, probably accusingly, at Lewin: he had to assume as much, it being difficult to tell from the wrong side of the pebble lenses.

Anna Spring, the fourth person present and seated at the oval table, looked deeply concerned as the speaker continued. 'It's not for myself, of course. I don't matter, and who knows it better, as many will tell you. It's for him who's gone over.' She paused. This gave Treasure the required moment to work out the identity of the subject and the permanence of the involuntary defection.

'It's not right, Mr Treasure. It's not right that the widow of such a respected figure should be accused of seeing things. It reflects.'

The lips tightened. The hands moved sharply to pull the unbuttonable cardigan across the massive bosom: again. The last action was symbolic only: the Ogmore-Davies upperworks were already decorously enough encased in high-necked flowered nylon.

'You're quite right, of course.' Treasure continued to steel himself: after all, he was paying a small enough price for the Judge's compliance over the Hutstacker deal. 'Mr Lewin and I'll go over the facts again and see if we can come up with a credible explanation.' He nodded confidently. 'The whole episode must have been very trying for you. But, you know, nobody doubts your word.'

'We talk about it every day. Never a day goes by without we talk about it.' Mrs Ogmore-Davies's gaze was now fixed firmly on the large, hand-coloured photograph of her late husband that hung above the fire-place. He was smiling and it would have taken little to convince Treasure that the grin had broadened in the previous half-hour. '*He's* always on about the body. *He* knows, of course.'

'Not coming through clear enough, is it, Mrs Ogmore-Davies?' It was difficult to tell whether Constable Lewin was being solicitous or sarcastic. He glanced towards Anna whose special regard he evidently courted.

'*They* can only lead us, Mr Lewin. It's not in the nature of things for *them* to tell.' It was a kind enough rebuke, giving Lewin the benefit of the doubt.

Mrs Ogmore-Davies now removed her glasses. Her eyes were closed and her hands she had placed palms downwards on the lid of a carved wooden box that lay before her on the table. There was an embarrassed silence in case she was communing with 'them'. After a few moments she sighed deeply, opened her eyes, and sadly shook her head.

'Ethel, I must go, I'm late already.' Anna rose and kissed the older woman on the cheek: this produced only grudging acknowledgement. 'I'm sure Mark will solve the mystery,' she added unperturbed. 'See you later, Mark. Oh, you coming too, Mr Lewin?'

'Duty calls, I'm afraid — or rather my other duties,' the policeman continued hastily as he climbed over several chairs. His supper break had started ten minutes earlier. 'See you again then, Mr Treasure.' He smiled at Mrs Ogmore-Davies and left, looking pleased to have escaped.

'Not the calibre of policeman you've been used to working with and that's a fact.' Mrs Ogmore-Davies, clutching the box, was herself now picking her way towards the door.

Treasure followed intending to take his leave and glad to quit the depressing room. There was no purpose in his insisting that he seldom worked with policemen, that he was a banker with really no business at Mariner's Rest. 'I'll be on my way then,' he said instead, but not before he had been guided to the sunlit sitting-room.

'Sit down a minute. This is for you, Mr Treasure.' A ready-poured glass of what he took to be sherry was thrust into his hand. Resigned, he settled on a deep, comfortable armchair near the open french windows. There was a magnificent and uninterrupted view of the bay. 'You felt the hostile vibrations next door? A very sensitive room, that is.'

Treasure smiled. 'I know very little about these things,

I'm afraid. This is excellent sherry,' which to a connoisseur might have suggested a second area of ignorance.

'I was trying hard to get help from loved ones passed over. Those close to me, and Anna, and the Judge even. They'd all want to help, you know.' She nodded confidently. 'They're all in here.' She touched the box that now lay on a table beside her.

Treasure tried not to indicate disbelief or mental discomfort. Recklessly he wondered whether the box might hold assorted ashes.

'Pictures, letters, little mementos,' Mrs Ogmore-Davies continued. 'Keep a wedding photo safe always, Mr Treasure,' she counselled earnestly, 'in case of need. They're best in my experience.'

The banker nodded seriously, wondering if he should go through the charade of making a physical note as a prelude to leaving. He leant forward earnestly.

'But there was hostility, Mr Treasure. And we know from which quarter. Oh yes.' The lips pursed bitterly. 'I'd shown Mr Lewin the little items I'd put in the casket before our meeting. Asked if there was anything he'd like to add. People often have little keepsakes on them.' She paused. 'Not interested or impressed. Prejudice and ignorance are nasty things. Closed minds some people have got, and that's a fact.'

'One meets it everywhere,' he agreed warmly, seeking not to prolong the exchange.

'But *he* was with us the whole time, of course,' she added unexpectedly.

'Who?'

'Captain Ogmore-Davies. Pouring his heart out he was. And not just about the murdered man I saw in the harbour.'

'Indeed.'

'Indeed, Mr Treasure.' The tall upright chair chosen by Mrs Ogmore-Davies offered a dominating advantage in the conversation. 'Contrary to what you may have been told, my late husband was not inebriated when he met his death. That came out clear at the inquest.'

'No one has suggested anything to me . . .'

'Well, Mrs Pugh at the Boatman wouldn't be above *implying*. That and other things. And it's not true. Sober as a judge he was when his heart failed. He might still have been saved, too, if he hadn't fallen back down those steps.'

The huge bird flew in dramatically out of the sun, skimmed Treasure's head, and settled, with a squawk, on the shoulder of Mrs Ogmore-Davies. The homing Gomer examined the visitor suspiciously first with one eye and then the other.

'The question the Captain is asking,' continued the formidable widow, leaning forward with enough of a jerk to agitate her feathered companion, 'the question he's asking *us*,' she embellished, unruffled by the wings flapping around her head, 'is did he fall, or was he pushed?'

'Oh Lord!' said Treasure, but under his breath.

'Pick a card,' said the Judge, 'any card.' He fanned out the pack he was holding towards Treasure who dutifully made his selection.

It was nearly seven o'clock, and the two men were standing at the drinks table in the drawing-room of New Hall. Thanks to the protracted interview with Mrs Ogmore-Davies, the banker had only that moment entered after bathing and changing at a furious pace. He had postponed his planned visit to the church, found he had forgotten to pack a favourite tie, and was in greater need of a Scotch and soda than a Nine of Diamonds.

'Put it back without my seeing it . . . That's it. I cut the pack three times . . . so . . . and shuffle . . . so . . . and *voilà*, your card, sir, was the Two of Spades.'

'Actually . . .'

'No, no, I see my mistake. It was this one, the—er—the King of Clubs?' Treasure shook his head. 'Wrong again? I think perhaps that trick's too advanced for me. Have a drink. Help yourself, my dear chap.' The Judge waved his hands over the array of bottles. 'How was Mr Ogmore-Davies?'

'Was it possible her husband was drunk when he died?'

'As a lord, I should think.'

Not for the first time Treasure considered how much satisfaction news of a drunken judge must bring to sober lords. 'But you don't know for a fact. I gather the coroner . . .'

'Gave him the benefit.' Nott-Herbert nodded. 'Drunk or sober, the fellow died of a heart attack. No point in stirring up gossip. Any special reason for asking?'

The banker decided to let this Parson Woodforde type summary pass. He shook his head. 'Those are very thick lenses Mrs Ogmore-Davies wears.'

'Thick enough to imagine things through?'

'Mm, I thought rather perhaps to make mistakes through.'

'It's been suggested. The problem is getting her to accept it. D'you think that's the answer?'

'It could be. Constable Lewin seems to think so. Anyway, I'm going to view the scene first thing in the morning.'

'Very good of you. Very good of you indeed to take this trouble. Come and see this picture,' the Judge added as though in compensation. He drew his guest towards the empty hearth and pointed to the large landscape that hung above it. 'Marcel Jefferys, Belgian Impressionist, oil on board. Magnificent, don't you think?'

'Quite beautiful and an unusual composition. He must deliberately have sat himself down with a silver birch a yard ahead and just off centre mucking up his view . . .'

'To paint the farm-house and so on a hundred yards

beyond. I thought the same thing. But it worked. Incidentally it's a larch not a birch.'

Treasure bowed. 'I stand corrected. I don't think I know Jefferys. The Belgian School of Impressionists . . .'

'Definitely Deuxième Cru but, like claret, not necessarily inferior for that.' He looked around the comfortable room. 'You'll find others of Anna's discoveries about the place. Nice little Cassatt sketch over there, for instance.'

Treasure walked over to examine the drawing. 'And the pictures in my room?'

The Judge pondered for a moment. 'The Utrillo's mine, bought by my grandfather. The Vuillard's one of Anna's. Like the Jefferys, it won't be here long.' He read the question in his guest's expression. 'It helps Anna if I take on some of her special finds for a bit. Keeps her capital from being tied up until the right buyers are about, and I enjoy having the pictures here.'

'I should think it also improves their provenance to have them come from the collection of Judge Nott-Herbert.'

'D'you think so?' The Judge seemed genuinely surprised and flattered. 'My grandfather was the collector, not me. I'm very small beer.'

'But you are a British Judge.'

'Oh, quite . . . quite so. I suppose Americans might . . .' The speaker stopped in mid-sentence. His free hand moved in a nervous gesture to the broad forehead. 'Americans. Americans. I quite forgot. We are about to be invaded by your friend Grabtop, or some such name, and Crutt, the most boring man on God's earth.'

'They're coming here?'

'My dear fellow, they should be with us already. There was a telephone message. Grabtop—'

'Crabthorne, I think.'

'That's it. Crabthorne and his wife are passing

through, staying the night at the gin palace up the road. Crutt rang to ask if he could bring them to call. He spoke to Mrs Evans, explained they were friends of yours. Since I was incommunicado rehearsing Stanley, she naturally invited them to dine.'

The 'naturally' implied that if in doubt Mrs Evans could safely extend Nott-Herbert courtesy and hospitality to all comers.

'Fortunately we're having cold salmon and we need to leave for the cathedral at eight-fifteen.' There was some doubt in the Judge's eyes as he pondered whether he had remembered to tell Treasure about the organ recital. 'They can all come with us. Do 'em good. So we shan't be put upon for too long,' he ended on an encouraging thought just as the peal of the New Hall door-bell echoed through the house.

Some minutes later Treasure was giving minimal attention to an earnest soliloquy from Albert Crutt, and feeling distinctly put upon.

Crabthorne's dissembling explanation of his presence in Panty offered on his arrival had been hardly softened by his insistence that he had tried to reach Treasure before leaving London.

It was plain the American had reason to be uneasy about the progress of negotiations over Rigley & Herbert — reasons the banker was certain would prove unfounded and which had almost certainly been invented by Crutt: who else?

Even now, as Treasure was obliged to countenance Crutt's loquacious drivel and to contemplate the appearance of his brassy-looking wife, he could hear Crabthorne loudly and unnecessarily promoting the benefits of a 'hands-across-the-sea' merger to the Judge, and for a variety of wrong reasons.

Patience Crabthorne, whom Treasure had met several times, had separated herself from the overt huckstering going on in the room by choosing to examine pictures on her own. Treasure liked Mrs Crabthorne: he abruptly excused himself to the Crutts and went to join her.

'Mark, I do believe that's a Mary Cassatt,' she offered.

'It is. Authenticated by a Judge.' It went through Treasure's mind he had just inadvertently acted out the purpose he had credited to Anna.

'We have several Cassatts in the University Gallery at home. She came from the next State, born Pittsburgh 1845, daughter of a Pennsylvania banker of French descent, friend and protégée of Degas. How's that for a newly enrolled docent?'

'Bravo. What's a docent?'

'A vulture for culture like me, ready to bone up on the exhibits in her local museum and then blind conducted parties with the dazzle of her enlightenment and erudition. Actually it's great fun.'

'Then kindly enlighten this ignorant party about what you're really doing here.'

Patience Crabthorne glanced at her companion in amusement. 'I'm here because your gorgeous and talented wife told me St David's was worth the trip. Edgar's here because that awful man Crutt thinks you're swinging the deal with the Judge and he needs Edgar to blow it by acting the Ugly American.'

'I thought as much.'

'I didn't, not until I met him when we arrived this afternoon. I really thought you were having problems and that Edgar might be able to help.' She looked across at her husband who was in full flight on the benefits of Ealing and dove-tailed production. The Judge appeared distinctly put-upon. 'I warned Edgar on the way here I thought he was being played for a sucker. If it's any consolation he'll figure it himself in a moment. He's not stupid, just impetuous. You're not offended, are you, Mark?'

'Not so long as I can put the pieces back when this little charade is over. Shall we intervene?'

It was at that moment that Anna walked into the room. She was momentarily surprised to see so many people but undeterred in her objective. 'Mark, you're a hero,' she cried, making for Treasure. 'I just heard on the local news how you defeated a gang of bandits on the train. Henry, did you know . . .' She had turned seeking the Judge, her voice faltered and faded as she caught sight of the man standing beside him. Crabthorne appeared equally nonplussed. There was a moment's awkward silence. Anna looked back towards Treasure and this time noticed the woman at his side.

It was Patience who broke the silence. 'Why it's Mrs Spring, isn't it? How very good to see you again, and such a coincidence.' She moved forward smiling warmly. 'Edgar, you remember Mrs Spring, her husband used to pilot your plane. My dear, we were so dreadfully sorry to hear of the accident—weren't we Edgar?'

Crabthorne was doing his best to recover his composure.

CHAPTER 11

He examined his forehea. in the bathroom mirror. Dusting the dried abrasions with complimentary Sunfun Tinted Talc did nothing to disguise the gunpowder wounds but it made him feel better. Thank God the swine missed burning his eyes.

He had heard the report on the radio news. Two armed men had assaulted and robbed passengers at Whitland Station. They had been resisted by a well-known banker, and a group of railway employees. The men had escaped *empty-handed* but had so far evaded capture.

So the police did have his luggage, which meant at some point they had had the passport. If he was to believe what he had just been told on the telephone the passport had since been 'liberated' and would be returned to him when he collected the money. Claiming the bag would be too complicated. Any communication with the police would be too complicated.

He walked back to the bedroom and began to dress. He had ordered dinner from the room service menu. He could have eaten in the hotel dining-room except the opposition hadn't figured yet where he was holed up and he was not going out of his way to tell them.

The Sunfun was hardly the obvious choice for someone wishing to pass unnoticed. Since the assault he figured he would be safer in crowded places. It had not been until after he had checked in he discovered the hotel was practically empty. The Filipino floor waiter had blamed this on the tourist preference for local hotels with Welsh staff: so much for whirlpools.

After making the second 'phone call, he was satisfied they had not been aiming to kill him on the train—just frighten him off. Even if they were lying they had the best of all reasons to keep him alive now. He had said that if he was not back in London after the weekend a letter would be posted immediately to Scotland Yard.

He wished he had floated that idea earlier. It happened not to be true but if he had known what he was running into coming here for a showdown it was exactly what he might have arranged.

As he unpacked the new blue shirt, he wondered who he might have trusted with such a letter. The sick feeling in his stomach came to match the bitter realization: there was no one—not any more.

In less than an hour he would be rich, and safely on his way to a secure future—but knowing he would gladly trade it all if there was some way out of this whole lousy deal. If only he knew a way back to square one.

Bitterly he thought back to the one other visit he had made to this place six months before. Such hopes he had nurtured then, such faith in his power to rekindle a relationship the ashes of which had blown in his face. And then that gruesome thing—to happen that night of all nights: the risk, his flight, the whole stinking episode.

Money-wise he was coming out on top, but it was no use fooling himself: he had lost the only thing that mattered in his whole life because he had trusted and been betrayed: because when he thought he was following he had just been left behind.

Positive thinking worked till the pills wore off: he had lost the whole bottle with his bag, and the chemist in Haverfordwest had refused to sell him more without a prescription.

He swallowed another neat Scotch and checked the time: it was just before eight. He had said he would be in the cathedral by 8.25 in the back row on the end seat next to the right-hand aisle. The whole row was reserved for ushers but wouldn't be used—like the six or seven rows in

front. He had checked earlier when he had bought his
ticket for the recital which began at 8.30. The acoustics
were bad in that section of the nave and the seats never
used at low attendance events.

Whoever brought the money would be in position by
8.20, two seats away from his with an unlocked attaché
case on the vacant chair between them. The case would
contain £100,000 in one hundred packs of £20 notes, plus
the passport.

The recital would last over an hour and he had made
the point he intended to count the money bill by bill. In
fact he had other plans, knowing it was scarcely in their
interests to try swindling him now. He knew they had that
kind of cash on hand and he had given them enough
notice on three-quarters of it. The caper on the train was
costing them £25,000, which meant they might have to
raid the pretty cash: hard cheese.

The whisky was providing the much needed fillip to his
confidence.

He had the perfect rendezvous—a private but visible
section of a public place with enough potential witnesses
around to underwrite his safety.

They would figure he'd be staying in the cathedral for
the half-hour at least it would take to count the money. In
fact he had just arranged with his unlikely accomplice to
be driven away at 8.30 on the dot. The car would be just
about as close to the cathedral door as you could get. He
had done his reconnaissance.

In five minutes he would leave his room and pick up
the taxi he had ordered to take him to the recital. He was
leaving his bag and the unwanted possessions—including
the stick—to imply he was returning. He had paid for a
night's stay in advance. In the manner of hoteliers he
would not be missed until noon the next day—hours after
he had been driven to Bristol Airport in time for the early
plane.

This time there would be no hitches, no waylayings, no knowledge of his plans or intentions. He was paying enough for the confidential service and for the protection—too much, perhaps, but there was everything at stake.

He looked at his watch again. He wouldn't enter the cathedral until 8.25 but it would make sense to be near the entrance soon and watch who was going in. He could do that incognito by just being himself!

For the third time that day he studied his new appearance in a mirror. The well-tailored suit had been sponged and pressed. The new shirt and tie were not exactly Bloomingdale's but they'd do. Above all he was through with clerical collars, wigs, false moustaches and phoney eye-glasses. He still missed the natural beard he had worn for years, but the short hair-cut suited him, and with £100,000 in his pocket . . . He smiled at himself and said aloud, 'Welcome, Mr Dylan Rees. Welcome to Provence.'

'For a cathedral that was destroyed in 645, sacked by Danes in 1078, burnt down in 1088, and fell down in 1220, I guess it's held out pretty well.' Patience Crabthorne was standing with Treasure and her husband at the top of the thirty nine steps that led down to the very much intact St David's Cathedral and its broad, lawned close.

'You forgot the earthquake in 1248.' Treasure was also managing without reference to a guide-book. 'Quite breathtaking, don't you think? From the west end to the High Altar wall I imagine it's substantially the same as at the end of the twelfth century, allowing for replaced breakages and some nice east-end additions.'

'Isn't that something?' Crabthorne was visibly impressed.

The steps commanded the perfect, elevated view of the cathedral from the south and east, together with the ruins of the old Bishop's Palace beyond to the west.

Treasure found it immensely moving to be gazing down on such a medieval gem in the deep hollow of the river valley where the Patron Saint had founded his church in the sixth century.

'I gather the inside is powerful and beautiful too. The outside I find almost muscularly Norman.' This was Treasure again.

'Inside it's awesome. There's no other word,' said the practised docent from West Virginia. 'I just let it humble me this afternoon when Edgar and his friends were indulging in the pleasures of the flesh. Shall we go down?'

Treasure had purposely arranged to join the Crab-thornes in their limousine on the short journey to the cathedral. Anna had gone ahead alone because of her involvement in the recital, but not before trying to dissuade the whole company from attending what she insisted would be a very boring occasion. For practical reasons the Judge ultimately chose to accompany the Crutts in their Jaguar Coupé.

On Patience's instruction Grouch, the driver, had deposited his passengers at The Popples, the wide pebble-stoned precinct at the end of the main street. Cars were parked there against the ancient wall that had originally and totally enclosed the cathedral area below. This gave the three the finest first vista of the cathedral but also the longest walk via the steps and a long path to the south porch.

Treasure had looked without success for Anna's white Honda among the parked cars. What he did note with amused surprise was Inspector Iffley's unmistakeable Mini-Estate. He assumed this was more an indication of the owner's predilection for Bach than the likely presence of dope fiends on ecclesiastical premises. He understood too it was possible to reach the main entrance to the building more closely by car on approach roads that

descended from the populated hill-top. These skirted the
cathedral area to the north and the south before finishing
close to the west end where parking was restricted. He
had heard the Judge instruct Albert Crutt to take the
north road 'and park by the Deanery' to save his legs.

Nott-Herbert had perhaps considered it more tactful as
well as physically less taxing to leave Treasure alone with
the Crabthornes on the scenic route. He had needed per-
suading, though, to join the Crutts, having at first
threatened to drive his own car to the recital on the score
that it was well-known to the police and thus easier to
park in prohibited areas.

He had made it fairly plain at dinner that he held Crutt
and Crabthorne in equal low esteem. Since common
courtesy suggested there was a larger obligation to suffer
even an unwanted visitor than to humour a kind of
employee, he had largely ignored Crutt and been grudgingly indulgent to the American.

Neither Anna nor Crabthorne had seemed pleased
about their unexpected encounter.

In contrast to her husband's attitude Patience Crabthorne had been especially warm towards the younger
woman, sympathetic about her misfortune, and full of
praise about the success attending her new life. She
handled the news of the engagement with all the understanding and sensitivity the delicate circumstances
demanded, earning the admiration as well as the
gratitude of Mark Treasure.

The banker was sure that whatever damage Crutt's intervention might have presaged to the progress of the
business negotiations had been spiked by Mrs
Crabthorne's civilizing influence. He firmly intended to
put the Judge's mind at rest as quickly as possible about
the unintentionally frightening presentation of Hutstacker plans retailed by Crabthorne, evidently at Crutt's
instigation.

It was certainly intended to phase out the relatively small Rigley & Herbert manufacturing plant in South Wales, and while it was true that few employees would be interested in moving to London, all were to be guaranteed first choice of jobs with the pharmaceutical and veterinary wholesale company already established by Rigley & Herbert at Llanelli and ripe for further development.

Encouraged by Treasure, Crabthorne had belatedly begun extolling the virtues of these plans at the end of dinner but at the time when the Judge was giving his complete attention to showing Patience how he could make a full glass of water covered by a napkin magically pass through a solid mahogany dining-table. Sadly this had soon involved Nott-Herbert in having to retire to change his trousers and Crabthorne had had no later opportunity to return to the subject.

Tactfully but firmly Treasure had made it clear in the car that it might be best to leave him to complete the job he had been asked to do with the Judge. Patience had boldly supported this suggestion, though it was clear that Crabthorne needed no encouragement about concurring.

'Mark, we're just here on vacation,' he commented with great bonhomie as the three strolled down the wide steps.

The cathedral, a hundred yards ahead and below them, was bathed in evening sunlight. The clock on the three-tiered square tower showed 8.20. People in surprising numbers were making their way towards the south porch where pathways from several directions converged.

'A creditable turn-out for an amateur organist,' Treasure observed as they drew near the entrance.

'It won't be oversold, and we've got reserved seats,' said Patience confidently. 'Go ahead. I'll follow in a moment,' she added stepping off the path on to the grass some yards short of the porch and making towards one of several ancient and crooked headstones: picturesque reminders of the ground's past usage, they served to punctuate the sward and probably to obstruct the labours of those employed to keep it trim. 'There's an epitaph here I saw earlier and meant to copy,' she called. 'Hey, don't get mowed down.'

Treasure glanced over his shoulder in the direction Patience was looking. The steps and path behind had suddenly become overrun by a rapidly advancing hoard of small, excited people.

Two coachloads of earnest and determined Japanese tourists were running late, chronologically and physically. They had arrived at the Sunfun Hotel at 7.30 instead of 5 o'clock and it was only thanks to the perseverance of the Sunfun Fulfilment Hostess ('available at all our locations') that they had been de-bussed, roomed, fed, watered and re-bussed in time to reach the cathedral, their next scheduled stop, not only at the original appointed time but with minutes in hand for many of them to employ taking photographs of almost all of them.

Although the cameras were in the main of the still kind, the photographers were moving, usually backwards, and it behoved anyone in the way not wishing to be involved in involuntary oriental group eurhythmics to stand aside or to move forward briskly. Treasure and Crabthorne increased their pace.

The banker was in front of the American when he came nearly face to face with the clergyman from the train. He recognized the man immediately despite the absence of the wig, the unconvincing moustache and any clerical accoutrements. Nor did it take the wound on the forehead to confirm the identity. It was the eyes.

The terrified expression in the eyes that Treasure remembered when he had found the fellow on the floor of the compartment—that same expression was there again, as if it had never left. The man staring at Treasure was beside himself with fright.

The entrance to the porch was only a pace away. There were two or three people between Treasure and a fellow being he charitably assumed was in need of help.

He stepped forward with his hands extended first to create a gangway and then to grasp the other man who appeared now to be pushing towards him.

The next moment Treasure found himself falling, toppled not by Japanese from behind but by two matron ladies maliciously as well as indecorously thrust into his open arms by the frightened man, and with such great force that Crabthorne too was brought down in the *mêlée*.

Treasure was able to catch sight of his late travelling companion turn about and run away from the upset of people he had created. With visual evidence of flailing bodies ahead at the very entrance to the cathedral the Japanese rushed to the conclusion that all seats were taken, including theirs: they also rushed the door.

Having already been deprived of a promised happy hour of huddled delight in a twelve-foot whirlpool, plus a complimentary drink, not to mention whatever part of their dinner had been intended to provide it with the gourmet status advertised, one hundred and twenty paid-up packaged travellers from Osaka did not intend to go short on plighted organ music. With cameras secured and the youngest members to the fore they advanced at the canter on a front both broad and deep.

Treasure was too concerned for the well-being of upset matrons either to note the ultimate departure route of the bogus clergyman (he had to be an imposter after pushing over old ladies), the disappearance of Crabthorne, or the immediate whereabouts of Mrs Crabthorne.

Some two minutes later the scene had changed. The last of the Oriental music lovers, still moving well, had vanished inside the still largely empty cathedral, a tribute to the motive power of group solidarity if not to the reliability of mass perception.

The toppled matrons were again making their way in the same direction none the worse for their shared tumble in the arms of a handsome protector but murmuring calumnies for the sake of appearance.

A straggle of genuine late-comers for the recital hurried past Treasure as Patience Crabthorne appeared beside him. 'What happened to Edgar?' he asked.

'I'm not sure . . . at least . . .' she hesitated deliberately. 'Let's go in or we'll be late.'

CHAPTER 12

Pushing the old women at Treasure had been a reflex action — in the split second when he realized who he was facing. He had to get out fast and unrecognized. The money could wait. All the money in the world could wait if he could just get away without that man seeing him.

He wheeled around and ran: ran for his life. He followed the path across the west end of the towering cathedral, crossed the narrow river by the small stone bridge, leapt down the steps on the far side and veered right at the corner of an outbuilding. Ahead was the road with the cars parked alongside the high wall on the left. Thank God there wasn't a single person in sight except the one he needed — standing as arranged by a white, two-door car under the tree on the right. He glanced back: there was no one following him, at least not yet.

'Quick. It's gone wrong. Got to get away.' His lungs were bursting. 'Had to leave the money. Tomorrow.'

The raincoated driver nodded, seeming to understand. A gloved hand opened the passenger door. The seat was already tipped forward. 'You'd best get in the back. Here, let me help.' Still the stage Welsh accent.

Too late he saw the sleeved weapon lift above his head. The sandbag cosh smacked across his temple flattening on impact and diffusing the damage of the devastating blow. With a rough heave the body was thrust face downwards into the back of the car.

The driver put the front passenger seat back in place, spread the rug over the still figure, slammed the door, then paused and looked around before walking to the other side of the vehicle. There was no one in sight nor again a few moments later when the car drove away from the cathedral and St David's, entering a familiar route of high-hedged lanes and cart tracks that in minutes would fetch up at the sea.

The figure who had stopped abruptly by the bridge in the shade of the outbuilding was bewildered but not alarmed at what he had witnessed. His eyesight was poor at the distance and he was not wearing his glasses. It seemed the car had been waiting under the tree, and the driver had helped the man get in. He was certainly too far away to pick up any of the conversation and instinct had warned him to remain where he was, unseen.

The conclusion he was drawn to was preposterous, he warned himself as the car sped away. Even so, if asked about the passenger's state of health, his reply might have been bizarre if not ambivalent.

'Let me take that.' Treasure indicated the bulging folio case that Anna Spring had just succeeded in zipping together.

She smiled gratefully. 'It's not really heavy. Just awkward. We sold more than a dozen drawings.'

The two were standing by a display table near the cathedral exit. As Anna had explained earlier, she had organized a sale of drawings donated by local artists to supplement the money raised at the recital for the organ restoration. This was why she had needed to arrive ahead of the others and why, the recital over, she and Treasure were nearly the last to leave the building.

'Were you sitting at the back? I couldn't see you.' He held the door for her.

'Mmm, we were still giving change from Japanese travellers' cheques when the music started. By the way, Henry took a lift with the Crutts, and I'm to drive you home. You enjoyed the recital?'

'Well enough, yes, but that organ certainly needs restoring. Albert Crutt sidled in at half-time. Whispered

he had trouble parking the car, and I would guess finding
a pub.' He snorted good-humouredly. 'They were sitting
just in front of us with Henry who dozed off during
"Sleepers Awake". Very droll. Ah, this is a new way for
me.'

They had turned right on leaving the cathedral and
were approaching the stone bridge dimly discernible in
the gathering dusk.

'You came down the steps,' said Anna. 'This is quicker.
My car is somewhere over there.'

'I suppose my demented friend ran off this way.'
Treasure shook his head. 'I'm glad he's alive and safe, but
I doubt if he's well.' He had already described the curious
happening before the recital.

'You're sure it was the same man—the one from the
train?'

'Pretty sure. I mean, he was dressed differently and had
lost his wig and so on, but he's a marked man, you know,
with that scarred forehead. I thought Crabthorne had
gone after him but he . . . he said not.' He had intended
keeping Crabthorne out of the conversation but the name
slipped in.

'The music was . . .'

'I should have known . . .'

They had begun speaking at the same moment to end
an embarrassing pause, only to invent another one. They
grinned at each other—like old friends: the uneasiness
disappeared.

'Edgar Crabthorne and I—'

'I don't need to know.' This time he had intended to
interrupt. 'It really is none of my business.'

'You're very English. Always the well-mannered protest. I appreciate it, and your sincerity.' She took his arm
unaffectedly, a measure of gentle intimacy—and of the
woman Henry Nott-Herbert was about to marry. 'I knew
Mr and Mrs Crabthorne during the little while Ralph was

their company pilot. It was before he'd leased his own plane.'

'And before you lived in Miami?'

'No, we were there already. Hutstacker's had a new plant nearby and they kept the plane there. Mrs Crabthorne didn't care for the area so didn't come down very much.'

'What about Crabthorne?'

'He was down a good deal, didn't know many people.' She shrugged her shoulders. 'Sometimes if he was stopping over a day or two he'd come to us for dinner, or we'd go swimming. He'd rented a beach cottage, I remember. He liked my husband's company.'

'Yours too, I'm sure.' There was more than gallantry in the comment.

'Perhaps. Ralph hoped Edgar might become a sleeping partner in the charter business we were planning. Put up some of the money, you understand?'

'And did he?'

'No dice, as the Americans say. But he was very good in pushing charters Ralph's way later on. Here's my car.'

'Allow me. Do you have the key? Oh, the door's unlocked.'

'With the key in the ignition. I was in such a hurry when I got here.' Anna looked lightly chastened by the reproving glance as Treasure helped her into the car. He got in the other side after putting the folio case in the boot through the also unlocked hatch-back door. 'I don't think they steal cars in St David's,' she added with mock innocence.

'Which makes it exceptional if not unique in the whole civilized world.'

They looked at each other and laughed. She placed a hand on his sleeve, and in the reflected light from a solitary and suitably aged streetlamp nearby he saw her expression change.

'I'm so glad you were there this evening when I walked

in on the Crabthornes.' She hesitated, looking for words, and he saw her eyes had suddenly filled with tears. 'It was . . . it was such a shock. I knew Edgar Crabthorne was involved in your business here with Henry, but I didn't know he was in the country. It brought back memories.'

'I understand.' She looked so dependent, and trusting, and so very, very beautiful. 'I didn't know they were here either until a moment before you arrived.'

'Could you make them go away? I have a special reason—and you are too gallant to ask what it is.'

He smiled. 'The sooner they're on their way the better I'll like it. Yes, I think I probably can get Crabthorne to understand he's gumming up the works by staying.' He was thinking of the American's effect on Nott-Herbert. 'Pity. Patience is good company, don't you think?'

Anna didn't answer the question. 'Thank you, dear Mark,' she said. Her fingers seemed to make tiny electric currents as they reached up to the base of his neck. Her hands drew his face to hers and she kissed him tenderly on the lips.

This seemed hardly the moment for philosophical cogitation but it went through Treasure's mind that it had been a singularly curious day.

'Sure I knew he was getting married—but not to Anna Spring.' The pyjama-clad President of the Hutstacker Chemical Corporation was standing before one of the twin washbasins in the bathroom of the Panty Sunfun Royal Suite, electric toothbrush at the ready and loaded with striped paste. He hesitated to begin operations at such a tricky point in the conversation in case he should place himself at a disadvantage.

Patience Crabthorne had no such inhibition. She had already finished brushing her teeth at the other basin and was examining her eyebrows in the long mirror that spanned the 'his and her' pink-tiled vanitory area. This also gave her the opportunity to gauge the degree of discomfort the topic under discussion might be causing her husband. Suspectful sidelong glances at one's partner's reflection had not been included in the inventory of 'togetherness' activities that came with the 'King and Queen' sized bathroom, but the arrangements allowed for this all the same.

'And Mrs Spring, or Anna as *we* came to know her . . .'

Patience was now gently massaging her forehead with cream from an expensive-looking bottle. She let the sentence remain uncompleted, allowing it to build atmosphere. Crabthorne continued to contemplate his toothbrush.

'. . . Anna may have known, I suppose, about your interest in . . .' Patience leaned closer to the mirror, '. . . I declare, that's a new wrinkle . . . heigh ho . . . yes, about your interest in Rigley & Herbert, or else her husband might have known.'

'Her husband was a fine man and a great aviator. May he rest in peace.'

Pleased with the knell of that pious incantation, Crabthorne began to clean his teeth. If there was anything you could count on with Patience, it was her sense of Christian charity.

'You don't have to be a Lindbergh to fly Lear Jets around Florida.' Wrong again: this biting sally came loud and clear over the buzz of the toothbrush. He pretended not to hear.

'I said you don't have to be a Lindbergh . . .'

He stopped the brushing. 'Yes, I heard you. Sometimes, Patience, I think . . . well, we'll let that go.' He shot her a forbearing glance. 'Sure, Ralph Spring may have known about this market hang-up we have over here. It's been a corporate pain in the butt for years. But he wouldn't have known we were planning to take over Rigley & Herbert. That kind of information you play close in.'

'You don't share it with company pilots . . . ?'

'Certainly not.' He rinsed and spat. 'Rigley's Patent Foot-balm,' he enunciated with venom, rinsed and spat again.

Patience was now smoothing the cream into her neck. '. . . or the wives of company pilots whom you could run into while their husbands were flying here, there and everywhere at your feudal bidding?' She gave a bland smile at the mirror before walking purposefully from the bathroom to the dressing-table in the matching pink bedroom, leaving her husband to consider the innu-endo—and a blob of toothpaste on his brand new Saks Fifth Avenue white pyjamas with blue piping.

She had come as close as ever she allowed to a direct reference to one of what she thought of as Edgar's 'little friends'—those who composed the group of executive employees' wives with whom he had enjoyed short-lived periods of amatory dalliance over the years.

Patience sometimes wondered whether the word 'en-joyed' properly described what Edgar drew from such liaisons: it had often occurred to her that far from being an indulgence, they had something to do with his fixation about close corporate relations and company loyalty: management monographs had been produced to prove the existence of even less credible syndromes.

No word had ever passed between Edgar and Patience Crabthorne on the subject of these extra-marital adven-tures: it was sufficient that she knew when one was pend-ing, happening and completed, the stages being reflected in her husband's disposition to demonstrate nervous an-ticipation, burdening guilt, and huge relief in that order.

She had long ceased troubling to identify the women involved, though it sometimes happened she found out by chance. Simply, she tended to take advantage of the burdening guilt phase to replenish her wardrobe, replace her car, or—selflessly—to exact a large tribute for her current favourite charity.

What could be termed Crabthorne's Syndrome had been quiescent until that very afternoon when Patience detected the onset of a nervous anticipation period brought on through the encounter with Mrs Crutt. She had suspected that nothing would come of this since she prided herself that Edgar had better taste.

The re-encounter with Anna Spring was something quite different: it fitted none of the phases though it absolutely confirmed in Patience's mind not only that Mrs Spring had been one of the favoured few but also one curiously able to agitate her husband long after the end of the affair. It was not in Edgar's nature to go back in any context, so what Mrs Spring had stirred was something other than a spent emotion.

'Patience, if you have anything on your mind . . .' Edgar had entered the bedroom determined to take the offensive.

'How much are you paying for this Rigley outfit?'

He shrugged his shoulders. 'Cash and stock around five million dollars. It's worth it. They have a whole lot of blocked assets besides their going brands. The hell of it is, but for Hutstacker competition they'd be worth peanuts. We built their market for them. Ten years ago we could have bought them out of petty cash.'

'And the Judge owns fifty-one per cent,' Patience interrupted. 'And pretty soon Mrs Spring is going to own one hundred per cent of the Judge. You know, Edgar, that kind of makes up for some of the tragedy in that young woman's life.' She gave an understanding smile. 'It's an ill wind that blows, or rather blew . . . where was it? . . . oh yes, in the Gulf of Mexico.' She looked about the room. 'I'd swear I put my book down in here.'

Crabthorne's gaze happened to fall upon the Gideon Bible on the bedside table. After today he hoped he'd never have to swear to anything that had to do with Anna Spring—or her husband.

CHAPTER 13

Early rising happened to suit Mark Treasure's consti-
tution. This subtracted nothing from his thinking of it as
an immensely virtuous habit.

'Good heavens, I must have got you up at the crack,
Mrs Evans,' he volunteered more heartily than apologetically, and much in the tone of a patronizing professional commending a good amateur effort.

'Ten to six you said, Mr Treasure, and there's no way
I'm letting you leave this house without something better
than the cup of tea you asked for.' She placed the half
grapefruit before him where he was sitting in lonely state
at the circular dining table. 'There's eggs, bacon, sausage
and kidneys under the silver dishes. I had plenty of time
to make kedgeree but not everybody likes it and I couldn't
very well wake you to ask' — advantage Mrs Evans.

She put a full toast-rack near his left hand. 'There's
terrible about the burglary. Ethel Ogmore-Davies could
have been murdered in her own home. Murdered or
worse. You never know these days' — meaningful nod.

'I thought she was out.' Treasure had finished the
grapefruit and was attacking the chafing dishes. With
such a highly civilized breakfast at stake, and only minutes
in which to consume it, postulating on anything so improbable as the ravaging of Mrs Ogmore-Davies was a
criminal waste of time.

'She happened to be out, it's true.' Mrs Evans was in no
hurry. 'Delivering parish magazines she was. Full marks
to Mr Lewin, anyway, seeing that window up — whatever
the reason,' she added uncertainly.

'Constable walking the beat. Backbone of the system,'
said Treasure with his mouth full and without real con-

viction. He was content to utter any palliating platitude
to forestall further discussion.

In any case, the subject's undramatic potential had
been exhausted at bedtime the night before. It had been
passed on to the Judge by his housekeeper that while he and
his guests had been consuming cold salmon the vigilant
Constable Lewin had come upon the invariably secured
dining-room window at Mariner's Rest standing wide
open to the lane.

Receiving no answer when he went to the front door to
make enquiries, Lewin had himself entered the house
through the open window, hoping to catch intruders red-
handed.

While searching the upper floor he had heard
movements below, but on noisily racing down the stairs
had succeeded only in terrorizing the just returned Mrs
Ogmore-Davies washing her hands, she said, in the back
lavatory: the door being half closed neither party had
been able immediately to identify the other.

Mrs Ogmore-Davies's reaction had been to slam and
lock the door, thrust her head through the tiny window
and scream for the police. This had placed her beyond
audible reach of Lewin's insistence that he was the police,
but not the sound of his heavy hammering on the door
which massively increased her perturbation. Having failed
to identify himself from inside, the policeman's only
recourse had been to rush outside and present himself to
the now nearly apoplectic Mrs Ogmore-Davies from the
trampled centre of her early lettuces. As a way of reducing consternation to mere vexation this had proved a
winner.

Later, a careful search of Mariner's Rest had revealed
nothing stolen or even disturbed—save a few chairs
knocked over in the dining-room.

Although the notion was steadfastly denied by Mrs
Ogmore-Davies, it had been assumed by most others, in-

cluding Lewin, that she had simply gone out forgetting she had opened the window to air the room after the meeting. Thus the Constable was excused the need to report the event to higher authority. Naturally, Mrs Ogmore-Davies and Mrs Evans had reported it to everybody available, the former being convinced the raising of the sash had been the work of an authority higher than any accounted on earth: a sign from beyond, but so far not pointing anywhere in particular.

'Ethel's a bit fanciful at times — over that kind of thing, I mean. More tea, Mr Treasure?' Mrs Evans was still hovering. 'Mark you, the warning about her husband's death was right enough. I can witness that.' The head nodded in baleful confirmation. 'Six stair rods removed and placed neatly on the kitchen table. Couldn't have been plainer for those with vision,' among whom presumably neither the speaker nor the gifted Mrs Ogmore-Davies could be numbered on that occasion. 'Come to think, it was Mr Lewin who found him, too. And Ethel was right about my Doreen, that's little Nye's mother.' She paused before adding, much to Treasure's relief, 'Well, that's another story. Doreen's married now. Not to the father and not what you'd call a prime specimen of a man, but still.' A sigh followed these painful admissions. 'Got their own house in Liverpool. Not Council,' she added pointedly. '*He* doesn't care for children . . .'

'How curious.' Treasure continued in his role as Greek chorus and reached for another piece of toast.

'Well, there's some like that, and to be honest Doreen doesn't either. Unnatural, I call it, even though she's my own daughter. Nye's happy enough though, living here with me. And he idolizes Anna. Haven't seen him yet, have you?' The proud glance suggested a treat in store.

'I don't think so.' Another half cup of tea and then he should make for the harbour.

'You will this morning, I expect. He and Emma, that's the vicar's daughter, Emma Wodd, they're up before anyone on Saturdays out playing and having picnic breakfasts. Did you ever?' Mrs Evans shook her head good-naturedly. Then the expression changed. 'Oh, I nearly forgot. His Honour told me to say if you wanted to take Devalera you're welcome. He usually goes with the children but a trained dog might be useful . . . in your investigations, like.'

Treasure wondered what Devalera could have been trained for. It amused him, too, that the Judge wanted it to be seen that the amateur investigation into an exceed-ingly cold case of suspected murder was being decked out with all available trimmings.

Even so, Treasure liked dogs and if this one was handy to keep him company and to add a touch of nobility—it was a grand sort of dog, after all . . . 'Where is he, Mrs Evans?'

'He'll be asleep in His Honour's car. I'll show you, sir.' She glanced approvingly at the nearly empty dishes.

Some minutes later Treasure was pausing after turning right half way down the High Street before what was evidently Anna Spring's picture gallery.

The noble Devalera was with him, responding impec-cably to the touches on the short leather leash. His handler suspected the good behaviour was solely attribu-table to the fact that they had taken the walk Devalera would have chosen himself. It remained that the dog added dignity as well as pace to the expedition.

Treasure had intended to trace Mrs Ogmore-Davies's walk on that Saturday morning two months before but had now decided there was nothing to be gained in tramp-ing down to the very foot of the hill. The harbour below had been partly glimpsed at various points along the way, as had the beginnings of interesting and tortuous-looking lanes and alleys that must lead to it.

The near-side of Anna's whitewashed pair of cottages provided a paved yard off the main road wide enough and more than long enough to accommodate her parked Honda.

The shop-front—new, but decently 'antiquated'—had no entrance directly on to the street. The common door to the commercial and domestic quarters was in the same little courtyard.

At its far end the yard funnelled into a sloping alley separated at the top by a low railing from some steps on the right. These plunged steeply to a house built at a lower level from those on the High Street: the alley itself followed a less perilous inclination.

Treasure had prolonged his examination of Anna's window display far longer than the unremarkable exhibits or his timetable justified. It was his intention now to take the alley down to the harbour, but he lingered in spite of his better judgement to humour the callow fantasy that Anna, sensing his presence, would greet him, all unexpected, from an upstairs window.

'Good morning. Lovely day.'

The voice was much too deep for Anna, and it came from behind. Treasure turned about and found himself confronting a cheerful postman pushing a bicycle with a sack on the front. Devalera, immensely pleased with the encounter, bounced forward a pace with Treasure, taken unawares, an involuntary leashed appendage.

' 'Morning, 'morning,' the banker replied, and then recklessly addressed the dog. 'Sit, boy. Sit.' Much to his surprise, Devalera obeyed instantly and proffered a pendulous paw to the postman.

'Got a way with dogs, I can see that, sir. How are you then, Devalera?' The postman, short and stocky, didn't have far to stoop to take hold of the paw. Devalera sitting seemed taller than Devalera standing: it was the way he stretched his neck.

'My name is Treasure. Would you be Mr Rees?'

'That's it, sir. Dai Rees. And you're the gentleman staying with His Honour. Welcome to Panty. Heard you had
a bit of trouble on the train. All right, are you?' The man
looked genuinely concerned.

Treasure chuckled. 'It was nothing,' he offered blandly.
'I'm more concerned about the trouble Mrs Ogmore-
Davies ran into at Easter . . .'

'With that old body in the boat.' Rees nodded. 'Funny,
that was. Never explained. Well, of course it wasn't or
you wouldn't be here, would you?'

'I might have been,' Treasure answered firmly. He was
still anxious to establish that unexplained bodies were not
his normal stock in trade—particularly with members of
that formidable band of citizens privy to the reason
behind the Judge's invitation. Even so, running into Rees
was a stroke of luck. 'I believe Mrs Ogmore-Davies met
you that morning.'

'On her way down to fetch Gomer. That's right. And
on this very spot. Not that she used this lane.' He
indicated the alley beyond. 'Nor ever would, of course.'

Begging dark questions seemed to be a local characteristic—Mrs Ogmore-Davies and Constable Lewin did it all
the time. 'Why not?'

'That's where the Captain met his tragic and untimely
death.' This bit of narrative was delivered with a rich
dramatic emphasis as the speaker pointed to the steps
that led down to the house on the right. 'Terrible thing to
happen. Put that light in since, the Council has.' He
pointed to a street-lamp bracket. 'Too late, of course.'

Treasure pondered this fresh information for a moment, then asked: 'Did you take this way down yourself?'

'That's right, sir. But not very far. Not to the harbour.
There's houses to left and right. Proper Hampton Court
maze it is down there. Been there I have,' he added

wistfully. 'Hampton Court Palace, I mean. There's grandeur for you. Seat of Henry the Eighth. Henry Tudor. See Britain first is my motto. You can have Majorca.'

Treasure smiled. 'So you're not the D. Rees who's lost his passport?'

'I don't have a . . . that is, I don't have much use for a passport.' Rees paused thoughtfully. 'Mrs Ogmore-Davies went straight down the main road after she'd told me about the parrot.' He reverted to the original subject. 'If you turn right at the bottom then you're on the flat along the water. That's the way she went.'

'And you didn't hear her shouting?'

Rees shook his head. 'Powerful voice she's got, mark you. Mezzo—nearly contralto. Solo calibre when young, so I'm told. But no, I didn't hear her. Terrible wind there was that morning.'

'And later . . . ?'

'Later, when she came to fetch Mr Lewin I was long gone. Counter-tenor, Mr Lewin,' he added gratuitously.

Treasure nodded. 'Any theory about what happened to the body?'

'None at all, sir. Unless it got up and walked away,' which, while offered as a joke, was exactly what Treasure was coming to believe it might have done.

The two men parted ways at the walled southern extremity of Anna's property, not far down the alley. Here the postman made off to the left past an iron gate to Anna's small garden and on a path that evidently led to habitations beyond.

Treasure, with Devalera close to heel, quickly reached the popple-stoned quay, the placid water of the inlet stretching before him from seawards on his right and past him, eastwards, up to the estuary of the tiny River Panty.

The hill behind him, crowded at the top with cottages, seemed even steeper when viewed from below than it had during the last part of the involuntary swift descent. There the lane had degenerated into an unmade path over rough ground — a short cut extending the paved section between the houses but not a route Treasure would have chosen even sober on a dark winter's night. He thought of Captain Ogmore-Davies and looked around for the Boatman Inn: it was twenty yards or so further along to seaward, tucked under the foot of the hill.

Opposite, across the water, ragged cliffs ran sheer down to the inlet. On that side there was no vestige of habitation except for sea-birds in the rock crevices — no human intrusion except the cliff-top walk, its line traced intermittently by the fencing that marked its more dangerous sections.

On that far side, seawards where the inlet narrowed, curving south, the short section of sea wall that made Panty half-tidal had been built out from the lower cliff face, leaving a narrow channel entrance to the harbour and marina.

Treasure was surprised, even mildly shocked, to note the virtual absence of yachtsmen about the place. There were boats in plenty, moored in neat lines on both sides of the long wooden pontoons, eight of which stretched out at right angles from the boardwalk below the quay wall. Most owners seemed happy still to be abed, wasting the sun and the blue sky: it was 6.30. Here and there a deck was being swabbed, a mast stepped, or a rope coiled, but still one had to search for such activity — something re-emphasizing in the banker's mind that Mrs Ogmore-Davies could well have been the only human being about at the matching time on a wet, dark Saturday morning two months before.

Treasure passed the Boatman and the Yacht Club — the first white-washed and picturesque, the other incongruously a replica of a Swiss chalet, all log cladding, a high-pitched roof, gable end facing the harbour with a wide balcony on the upper floor. Although obviously a cheap, prefabricated edifice intended for a quite different environment, the Panty Yacht Club still had a kind of impertinent charm about it.

Devalera was more interested in the far end of the quay. He was tugging at his leash. Treasure, who had been asked only to prevent the animal dislocating traffic flow in the High Street, felt there was no danger in allowing him to take a swim, and so undid the leash.

It was not the water the dog had been craving. He made off at great speed towards what Treasure guessed was the long disused lifeboat station, a building standing well beyond the others, its seaward end surmounting a stone slipway and its rear cut into the hillside. It had a venerable look and must once have housed at worst a cutter with double banked oars or at best a steam pinnace. Behind and higher on the hill-side were the remains of what might have been a small winding shed. The tarred and slated roof of the main building was saddled at the back almost certainly to allow access for cables from above used to winch the lifeboat up the slipway.

The dog had scrambled up the hillside and was now standing athwart the roof of the lifeboat station where he had paused to give a full-throated rendering of his penetrating and fatiguingly predictable slow-tempo bark. It was clear he was addressing himself to the winding shed and, much more surprisingly to the watching Treasure, had done so with almost immediate effect.

The shed had no roof, but its sides had survived. One could just make out a small scowling face that had appeared above the front wall.

But the voice came from much closer by. 'Excuse me. Do you think they're in trouble?'

The skinny barefoot teenaged girl had diverted Treasure's attention by calling up to him from where she was standing below on the boardwalk. She put down the red plastic bucket and pointed towards the entrance channel to the harbour. A small fishing-boat with an outboard motor at maximum throttle had appeared and was heading towards the quay.

'Chap in the stern looks a bit agitated,' Treasure replied.

'The one waving? That's my brother. They went out crabbing early. Listen, he's shouting something . . . it's . . . listen.' They both did. 'He's shouting fetch a doctor.'

'Well, don't worry,' said Treasure, 'he looks healthy enough, and so does the other one.'

'That's his friend. Do you think . . . ?'

'Why don't you belt off and 'phone for a doctor as your brother says.' He could now see into the boat from where he was standing. There was an ominous shape covered in tarpaulin on the centre thwart which the girl could not have seen from sea-level.

'Right,' she said, dropping the mop alongside the bucket. 'Won't be a tick.'

Treasure called Devalera and without waiting to see if the dog responded took the nearest steps down to the waterside. The young man was heading the boat to come alongside at the old lifeboat slipway. Treasure was there waiting when he did so.

The two visible occupants of the boat were worried-looking schoolboys of fifteen or sixteen, older and for the moment much paler than the girl. The body of the swimmer under the tarpaulin was icy cold, heavily lacerated, and very dead.

'I don't think we'll need the doctor,' Treasure said gently and re-covered the body.

'We found him in the next bay. It's very rocky . . .'

'We tried reviving him. I thought a doctor . . .'

The two lads had begun speaking rapidly at the same time.

'You did all the right things, I'm sure.' Treasure glanced

at his watch. 'Either of you know where the village policeman lives?' Both boys nodded. 'Well, it happens he's supposed to meet me here in ten minutes. Why not run and ask him if he could come now? Tell him what's happened and that we'll need an ambulance. I'll look after the boat. Oh, and head your sister off, there's a good chap.'

The boys left immediately, which gave Treasure the opportunity to lift the canvas again.

The body clad in swimming trunks seemed to have been terribly beaten about. One arm was hideously twisted, there was a deep gash across the chest, and the lower face was badly disfigured.

What Treasure needed to re-examine was the small surviving dried-up wound on the forehead—that and the platinum wristwatch.

CHAPTER 14

'Treasure saw him too.'

'What d'you mean too? We can't be sure the others did, and we'd allowed for Treasure.' He was aiming to soothe but it just wasn't his style with early morning telephone calls. Thank God he'd made the coffee. 'If he'd told us what day he was coming instead of acting so bloody scared we could have stopped him meeting Treasure in the first place.'

'But you found out . . .'

'When they were both cosied up in the same compartment. You'd warned him about Treasure, for heaven's sake. Anyway, what's the point in . . .'

'Probably he thought it was safer to be here the same time as Treasure. The point is he had every right to be scared. He could have been killed.'

'No, he couldn't. Honestly he couldn't.' This needed very delicate handling. 'All right, so it was a mistake to try frightening him off.'

'It was tawdry.'

'OK, it was tawdry but it could have saved us a packet if it'd worked.'

'We didn't need to save . . .'

'All right, all right. So last night he'd have got everything he wanted. It was lousy luck you never had the chance to turn him back, and I never knew we needed to. If I'd just found out where he was staying. And with only that dimwit helping you at the cathedral.'

'He may be dim but we should be thankful . . .'

'Agreed. Agreed. Your car was there?'

'Sure. Pity you weren't. Anyhow, the woman who rang just now . . .'

'I just can't figure where he's picked up a woman . . .'

'The woman said my American friend would meet me at the gate of New Hall at three to pick up the present, or else send a messenger. If it was a messenger the password was Windsor Castle.'

He sighed audibly. 'That's half an hour after the gardens open to the public?'

'Yes. There are notices all over the village.'

'With the lovely Anna taking the money at the gate.' He paused. 'Another crowded place where he thinks we won't molest him. Hell, he came down here to negotiate, to make a deal. Now he knows he's getting the lot, passport and all, why run the risk of being seen . . .'

'Because he thinks it's safer and because he doesn't trust us.'

'Well, I don't like the messenger and this fool password bit.' He paused. 'Still, if it's the only way to get him out of our hair short of . . .'

'Short of what?' The question came too quickly.

'Short of nothing. I'm just kidding. Really I'm sorry for him.'

'I think he'll be there himself.'

'With a hundred thousand at stake I'd be there too.'

'Treasure could be around, but the others . . . God, there's someone waiting outside. I'll have to go.'

The 'phone at the other end went down with a bang. He shook his head. Perhaps His Honour was paying his respects.

He drained the coffee cup and went back to gazing at the oil painting propped against the milk jug. It had been worth the night drive to Cardiff and back just to be looking at it, even with everything else that was going on: you could easily get hooked on this art business.

The strictly unregistered dealer had been genuinely loath to part with this one at bargain prices—but he accepted you had to spread the stuff about: he got so much of it since the advent of the various capital transfer taxes. The picture was so good, though, it seemed incredible the previous owner had dared leave it uninsured and undocumented. Anyway, given a fresh provenance, catalogued as 'Dutch School' with an informed and not too outrageous hint about which Dutchman, it would fetch an easy £10,000 in London.

He smiled to himself: all he had been after was caches of LSD—it was funny how one thing had led to so many others. He looked at the time. It was still only 6.30.

'It's well placed strategically for a look-out post.' Treasure believed it important not to talk down to children.

'What's strategically?' asked Nye.

'We play look-outs,' said Emma.

'And tanks and hospitals,' Nye added quickly.

The three were sitting inside the remains of the little winding shed which lacked a back wall as well as a roof. Devalera was asleep on the hill nearby.

Treasure smiled. 'You come here every Saturday?' He was glad the need to define 'strategically' seemed to have lapsed: he wondered how the dictionaries put it. 'Must be jolly cold in winter, and dark too.'

'Not every Saturday. And we're not supposed to come here at all. You won't tell?' She was 'Alice' in a junior boiler suit. 'We're not afraid of the dark.'

'*She* is sometimes, but she's better than most girls. She doesn't mind spiders. I've got a kissing-ring.'

'A chrysalis,' Emma corrected mechanically.

'In a match-box,' Nye ended, undeterred.

It was half an hour since the dead body had been taken away in the ambulance. Constable Lewin treated drowned swimmers with the practised tolerance of the seaside policeman duty bound regularly to note the visibility, legibility and stability of signs about dangerous bathing. It was not a local man, he had said, and most likely a visiting enthusiast for sea bathing, cold water, and rock clambering. The incoming tides were something cruel in the rockier coves.

The victim had been assigned to the nearest pathology unit and Lewin had immediately prepared to leave to make his report and to check on missing persons. He begged Treasure's pardon for having to postpone their intended further consideration on site of Mrs Ogmore-Davies's awful experience, adding the loyal parochial comment that it was good there had been so few visitors around to witness the morning's tragic catch—such things being bad for trade.

Treasure had volunteered the drowned man had resembled someone he had been involved with on the train the day before, and who had also been wearing a distinguishing platinum watch. The last comment had surprised the policeman who had listed the watch case as aluminium: the point had been duly corrected. No, Treasure had not been able to state with assurance that this was the same man, but if it was, then the Haverford-west police might have the means to identify him.

Lewin had recorded all this before leaving, signifying with a pomposity that perhaps belied the truth that he had heard all about Treasure's train adventure from top police sources, not just through listening to the local radio station. In reply to Treasure's casual inquiry about whether the passport found at New Hall had been claimed, the constable said no such document had yet been delivered to him. The banker had hesitated to suggest that it could have belonged to the dead man, there being a limit to the elaborations on unsupported supposition he felt entitled to unleash on a village policeman.

The children had been standing with the small group of people gathered in time to watch the ambulance's departure. Treasure had guessed their identities through Devalera's movements: the dog had sat himself between them watching events with an interest that matched their own, and from nearly the same eye level. They were obviously trusted and preferred familiars.

It was at Treasure's suggestion that all four had climbed the rocky way up the side of the lifeboat station to the outpost they now occupied, from which, the children had to admit shamefacedly, they had tried to steal down earlier unobserved — an event precipitated and advertised by the barking of their canine associate.

'I'll bet you were here Easter Saturday morning.' This was Treasure playing a long shot.

'Why?' the two asked in unison.

'Because you'd have had buttered hot cross buns for picnic breakfast instead of jam sandwiches like today. Would have made up for the weather.'

'We've got a tin roof we use if it's raining and . . .' Nye's blooming enthusiasm withered under Emma's warning glance. 'And . . . er . . . and only if we come,' he finished limply.

'Were you playing look-outs that morning? It was a bit drizzly.'

Emma broke the awkward silence that followed. 'Submarines,' she said a trifle grudgingly.

'You see we've got this penny thing . . .'

'Periscope.'

'. . . that lets you see right round without anybody seeing us. You can see right up to the street and down to the boats.'

'And did you see the man who frightened Mrs Ogmore-Davies?'

This time the silence was even more awkward and prolonged. 'Yes.' It was Emma who took the plunge. 'But we weren't supposed to be here. Will you tell on us?'

'You're a detective, aren't you?'

'Sort of.' Treasure smiled.

'Told you,' said Nye triumphantly.

'But I won't tell on you if you explain what happened. Promise. I'll say I worked it out.'

'Will they believe you 'cos you're a detective?'

'Yes. Anyhow they'll have to.'

'He came from Idris Lane.' Emma sounded relieved.

Treasure frowned and then he remembered. 'That's the lane that runs down the side of Mrs Spring's house? Can you see it from here?' He looked back, tracing the direction he had taken to reach the harbour. 'Yes, you can. The top of it anyway.' He could even see the back gate to Anna's garden.

'He came running down like you and Devalera this morning, only he had no clothes on . . .'

' 'Cept shoes.' Nye's contribution.

'Except shoes. He was carrying his clothes in a bundle and running very fast. He jumped off the quay on to the boarding below where you can't be seen . . .'

' 'Cept from here.'

'And he was trying to put his clothes on when the whole lot blew in the water.' Emma continued.

'It was ever so funny.' Nye was still smirking at the memory, rocking backwards and forwards, arms clasped around his knees.

'He was fishing them back with a stick when Mrs Ogmore-Davies came.'

'We hadn't seen her either.'

'We were watching the man when we heard her. He heard her too and saw her and just kept ever so still hoping she wouldn't see him . . .'

'Or go away.'

'And she did,' said Treasure. 'Did he have the stick tucked into his arm?'

'Mm. Mrs Ogmore-Davies thought he was stabbed, she said after.'

'But he wasn't?'

Emma shook her head. 'As soon as she'd gone he fished

out his clothes and ran up behind the yacht club. Then he got dressed and went up High Lane—that's the one nearest.' She pointed to some steps that evidently terminated the alley indicated at the harbour end.

'And you saw Mrs Ogmore-Davies come back with Mr Lewin?'

Both children shook their heads. 'We didn't know about that till later,' said Emma, 'about her thinking it was murder and everything. And we couldn't say because we hadn't said in the first place. And Daddy had said . . .'

'You shouldn't come here.' Treasure wondered how he was going to explain the story away while keeping his promise to the children. It then went through his mind that since there had been no murder, or anything on the face of it approximating even to an accident, there was no obligation moral or practical to explain anything to anybody.

He was speculating hard on why a naked man should choose or need to race to a harbour at just after six on a wet April morning. Joggers wore clothes: streakers were out of fashion—and season.

'How old d'you think the man was?'

'You don't know?' A surprising comment from Nye who possibly assumed detectives deduced that kind of thing.

'Pretty old,' said Emma.

'Younger than you.' Nye again.

'Yes, much younger than you.'

'But pretty old,' Treasure echoed amiably.

Obviously the man had been quite young, certainly athletic, quick thinking and a practised judge of human reactions—or at least a lucky one when it came to making a snap decision on the likely course of Mrs Ogmore-Davies when exposed to a shocking situation. The simulation of the stab wound had been a brilliant piece of improvisation. Of course one ought to be outraged, but somehow . . .

The role of the surprised but resourceful lover seemed

more and more to provide the solution—indeed, in Treasure's mind, the whole sequence was now taking on the character of a French farce on outdoor location.

'You didn't see where he came from in the first place? Er . . . whether he came from the High Street, out of a house or . . .' He hesitated to add anything about bedroom windows or drainpipes.

Both children were shaking their heads.

'We saw what he did after.' This was Nye.

'Well?'

'He got in his car half way up High Lane.'

'It was parked up there? What sort of car was it?'

Nye and Emma exchanged questioning glances. It was Emma who answered eventually. 'It was a Mini.' She took a deep breath before continuing. 'It was the one he was driving yesterday when he brought you to New Hall.'

CHAPTER 15

'And you are seriously suggesting, Mr Treasure, I should let the whole thing drop? Pretend that it never happened?' Mrs Ogmore-Davies sounded less incredulous than her words might have suggested.

Treasure had joined the widow at her breakfast on the little terrace outside her living-room. He had gladly accepted a cup of tea.

'As I said, what you saw was play-acting. I can give you my word no one was hurt. The man you saw never intended you to think he'd been stabbed. He was involved in some very hush-hush activity . . .'

'Official. To do with the drugs, you say.'

He nodded. 'He didn't want to . . . er . . . implicate you—in your own interests. It could have led to your being called as a witness. That sort of thing.' He gave a pained look. 'Best to steer clear if possible.'

'What about the police? They must have been involved. Mr Lewin . . .' She placed her finger unerringly on the weakest spot of a fairly feeble st \ cture.

'Yes. Lewin.' Treasure paused. He hoped that if he waited long enough . . .

'Of course. I see it now.' Mrs Ogmore-Davies was happy to write her own scenario when it came to Lewin's part in the affair. 'He'd have known no more about it than me. Special people they have for that kind of work. Not village bobbies.' The expression turned conspiratorial. 'Told you what I thought of him yesterday. Then on top of that there's what I said about the burglary.' She leant back in a gesture of triumph, lips pursed. 'Definitely second rate. Stands to reason *he* wouldn't have been part of anything secret.'

Treasure allowed himself the merest nod signifying

affirmation of, if not implication in, the character assassination of the hapless Lewin. 'I've no doubt he does an adequate job according to his abilities.' He smiled knowingly over the tea-cup.

'But he'll still think I was seeing things.'

Treasure was prepared for this one. 'I think not, at least when the powers-that-be have had a word.' He had the Judge in mind for this key role. 'I believe you can rely on it, Lewin won't ever refer to the thing again.'

'And the gossips? The wagging tongues in this village, Mr Treasure. You wouldn't believe.'

'Will be stilled by your exemplary and mature attitude in making it known you have closed the subject.'

'In the public interest.'

'One could assume that, certainly. It would be in nobody's interest—' and here he was anxious to fold in the best interests of Mrs Ogmore-Davies herself—'really not anybody's, to know you were down there alone with a perfectly healthy . . . er . . . naked young man. Difficult.' He adopted his most judicious expression reserved usually for the client whose rejected take-over bid had better be decently abandoned and not wantonly improved out of pique and in defiance of sound economics. 'Could open another tin of worms.'

Mrs Ogmore-Davies had been thinking along the same lines. 'Not fair really, but I suppose by not demeaning myself . . .'

'How right you are, Mrs Ogmore-Davies. Rather like the war, I expect. No doubt with a husband high up in the merchant marine . . .'

'Several times Convoy Commodore.'

'Exactly. You must have been privy to secret information more important . . .'

'Say no more, Mr Treasure. If Ethel Ogmore-Davies can help the authorities by keeping mum, then so be it. More tea?' The healthy, naked young man had done the trick.

Treasure passed his cup. The widow had not pressed him as to the highly confidential source of his information. She made it plain she considered it was both reliable and in some wonderful way available to him and not to others — which in a sense was true.

So the children and Mrs Ogmore-Davies were silenced for differing but enduring reasons. Lewin would need no reason at all when asked never to mention the matter again, which disposed of the obvious principals. Inspector Iffley did not count in the present context, even assuming the children had been right in their identification — something Treasure intended to muse upon later. For the moment he was much too anxious to test a theory before leaving Mariner's Rest.

The children and Treasure had returned from the harbour by different routes. Devalera had been turned over to Nye's keeping. Treasure had been warmly received by the Captain's widow even though 8 a.m. was an unfashionable hour for social calls. He had been offered breakfast but had taken only tea immediately after being shown the site of the previous evening's break-in — not that there was anything to see. There were certainly no signs of forcible entry.

Now he rose, and with tea-cup in hand, sauntered across the narrow lawn to pay his respects to Gomer. The bird was treading its perch at the entrance to the greenhouse.

' 'Morning, Gomer,' he said affably but with no expectation of response: even if the bird talked it wouldn't do so for him — they never did. 'A pretty creature,' he remarked turning his face back towards Mrs Ogmore-Davies. The bird took the unguarded opportunity to strike out viciously at Treasure's hand, missed, and fell off the perch with much squawking and flapping of wings before righting itself again.

The banker smiled, returning to his seat at the table.

Somewhere he had read that a parrot's bill closed with a force of 350 pounds to the square inch. Since then he had been careful always to stay out of immediate pecking range.

'Naughty Gomer! Bad Boy!' Mrs Ogmore-Davies was confused and abased—fulfilling the object of Treasure's diversion.

'Did the burglar steal what was in that box you had at our meeting yesterday?' Very carefully he watched her reaction to the unexpected question.

'My photos, you mean? Why on earth should anyone want those?' The surprise was obviously genuine. There had been no pause for calculation. Mrs Ogmore-Davies was clearly baffled.

'Have you looked in the box since the meeting?'

She rose, walked to the sitting-room, and returned with the box. 'We'll soon see. It's not locked. There's nothing . . .' The voice faltered, then sank to a whisper. 'There's nothing in it. Well, did you ever?'

Treasure had walked right around the outside of the church. Now he charged himself to do the same thing again—this time paying attention to what he was seeing.

It was Detective-Inspector Iffley who had been occupying his mind to the exclusion of stepped gables and a host of what he would normally have considered equally absorbing features of venerable architecture.

Iffley had confided he was engaged in unusual work: the man's appearance and equipment had indicated that much. There would be no predicting a day's events—or a night's either. You would need to be fast-thinking, adaptable, tough—definitely tough to cope with whatever circumstance forced upon you.

Treasure was familiar with the brilliant coups achieved in uncovering drug-trafficking rings. The seeds of these successes must be sown by the lonely, heroic and dangerous work of men like Iffley. The Inspector had modestly explained he was just doing a clearing up job: 'clearing up' could be self-effacing euphemism.

The Inspector had emphasized his work kept him inland, but it could hardly do so exclusively. His car had been in St David's the evening before, unless Treasure had been mistaken—but it was such a distinctive car.

Of course, the children could have been mistaken too about the man—*and the car?* They had described both with remarkable accuracy.

No doubt duty had brought Iffley to Panty that night two months before. And who could question that the drama of his departure had not been bound up in some anti-criminal activity? Treasure tried to put from his mind that frivolous, unfair speculation about a scene from a French farce.

Mrs Ogmore-Davies had provided a meticulous description of the inhabitants of Idris Lane and its immediate tributaries. This had not been difficult: it was a piece of Old Panty still occupied in the main by folk who had lived there for years—retired couples and old ladies all well known to the Captain's widow. And there was not a nubile daughter, a young wife. neglected or otherwise, indeed any female under the age of seventy among the lot—except the one that Treasure knew about.

If he was interested in buying property in that particular section (the spurious reason he had offered for his inquiry) it had been Mrs Ogmore-Davies's opinion, complete with sniff of disapproval, that Anna's house would be the first available following her marriage—not that he would want a shop as well. So Anna really was the odd one out.

No, he mused, if he had been buying a weekend place he would not want to sell pictures, or antiques, or—he called to mind the phraseology—the lower grade bric-à-brac that was the stock in trade of Iffley's cover job.

He was recalling, too, that tender embrace in the car. It had been a spontaneous expression of gratitude—a pure acknowledgement in an unexpected kiss—which he had enjoyed (very much indeed) and which he had persuaded himself had been an endearment as innocent as it was rare.

'And who do you think you're kidding?'

Treasure swung around. It wasn't the voice of conscience: it was the Vicar which, in a sense, was close enough.

'I'm so sorry,' said the genial clergyman who had emerged head bent from the church door. 'Hope I didn't startle you. Wasn't expecting anyone. Practising my lines for this afternoon. Well, it's only one line actually but I'm not supposed to move my lips when I say it.' He paused uncertainly. 'I expect you think I'm loopy.'

'Not at all,' Treasure replied with great good humour, 'I suspect you are somehow involved with Henry Nott-Herbert and a ventriloquist's doll—I mean dummy.'

'You too?' said Emma's father. The Reverend Handel Wodd was of middle height and weight, thirty-five or so, moon face surmounted by a shock of unparted, curly brown hair and adorned with round, old-fashioned, gold-framed spectacles: it was a humorous rather than a studious countenance. 'I'm a mysterious voice from an unexpected quarter. Henry conjures me out of nowhere, if you follow me.'

'I think so. My name's Mark Treasure.'

'I thought it must be. Sorry we didn't meet last night. Yacht Club meeting. Kept me all evening.' The voice had a melodious Welsh lilt. 'You'll want to see the church, I know.' He looked at his watch.

It was still quite early and it occurred to Treasure he was about to be offered yet another shared breakfast. 'Which I can do any time. Have you eaten yet?'

'Yes, before I said Matins.' Cheerfully the Vicar nodded

back towards the church where he had probably been reciting the morning Office by himself. 'I've half an hour before I'm booked to instruct a shortly to be married couple on raptures unforeseen. Let's start with the tower. Terrific view from the top. You good at steep stairs? It's not that high—just awkward.'

Treasure enjoyed the church of St Dogvan. He marvelled at the literally indestructible thirteenth-century tower at the west end with walls three feet thick, saddleback roof, slit windows the whole broadened at the base—all pre-dating the rest of the church and built as a haven and stronghold against marauders from the sea.

He enjoyed the tacked-on narrow fourteenth-century nave built in less troubled times, the perversely asymmetrical and widening chancel that came later complete with the grand Perpendicular east window. He even smiled upon the twentieth-century Gothic transept to the north—the gift, the plaque made plain, of Henry's grandmother, in memory of one who, judging from his taste in houses and fine art, should have commissioned the job himself while he was able.

Altogether it was an agreeable muddle of styles, fit-ups, floor levels and masonic compromises, something Treasure infinitely preferred to churches built of a piece which show less the changing fortunes of the generations that come and go around them.

'You know, it's believed more than twelve thousand bodies were buried in the churchyard over the centuries.' The Vicar had proved a mine of information on his church. 'It's not that big either,' he added. 'Mark you, they never allowed interments inside, under the floor, not like the London churches.' There was a touch of pride at the end.

'Twelve thousand. Would that be a matter of record or intelligent supposition?'

'Mostly record, certainly over the last three or four centuries. Meticulously preserved Burial Registers. Like to see some?'

Treasure nodded enthusiastically. 'When you're not so busy. Tell you what I would like a sight of—your Baptismal Register of thirty-five years ago.

'That's easy. It's right here.' They were standing in the chancel and the Vicar led the way into the vestry which was close by—part of the 'new' north transept. 'Any special reason?'

'I wonder if a Dylan Emrys Rees, 35 today and born here, was also baptized . . .'

'Easier still. He was. He still lives here. He's our choirmaster—Dai Rees the postman.' Wodd was turning back the pages of a record book he had taken from the vestry safe.

'But I thought Dai was the common Welsh contraction of David . . .'

'Or Dewi or Dafydd but not Dylan. You're right. The thing is, Dai Rees was christened Dylan to favour the poet, but his mother went off Dylan Thomas later.' The Vicar shrugged his shoulders. 'I've no idea why. The family used to be strict Chapel and probably teetotal another generation back. Perhaps Thomas's drinking was too much for Dai's mother to tolerate. Anyway, Dai he became, and Dai he stayed.'

'How very interesting. I met him this morning.'

'Lovely man. Do anything to help a friend. Tower of strength in the church. Strong convictions, too. Pacifist, as a matter of fact. Funny, I couldn't have told you about the name business until a few months ago. I've been Vicar here six years and until Dai needed a passport I always thought his proper name was David.'

'He got you to countersign the form and witness his photographs?'

'In January it was. "I certify that this is a true likeness of Mr Rees" and so on,' the clergyman quoted with a sigh. 'The law says it can be done by a Member of Parliament, a Justice, a lawyer, a doctor and any number of other worthies who people don't like to trouble. But it's always the poor parson they come to. Odd though, in the case of Dai he's never been anywhere, not abroad I mean, nor ever likely to go from what I can gather. Takes his family holidays visiting the Queen's and other people's stately homes.'

'He told me they'd been to Hampton Court.'

'And Longleat, Wilton, Windsor Castle and I don't know where else. Here's the entry.' Wodd pointed to a place in the register. 'Looks as though he was baptized two Sundays after his birth in strict observance of the rubric in the old Book of Common Prayer. Very conscientious people the Welsh — even converted Nonconformists.' He laughed.

It was possible but highly improbable that two people destined to be named Dylan Emrys Rees had been born on the same day in the same tiny village. Treasure searched the Register backwards and forwards without result.

It was conceivable also that the second Dylan, if he existed, could have had Roman Catholic, Nonconformist, or non-believing parents in which case he would not have been baptized into the Episcopalian Church in Wales: the Baptismal Register was not conclusive.

Was credulity stretched a sight too far when one learned both alleged D. E. Reeses must have obtained new passports issued in the previous February? The chosen answer to this question was what allowed conviction to replace objective scepticism in Treasure's mind.

No amount of inexpert or purposely fumbled photographic work could explain the total dissimilarity between the image of D. E. Rees contained in the passport and the face of D. E. Rees that had beamed upon Treasure earlier in the morning. If only one D. E. Rees existed, then the passport the banker had seen on the previous day was fraudulent.

Why, Treasure asked himself, had honest, God-fearing Dai Rees, postman and choirmaster, chosen to hoodwink the authorities, and—not to dissemble—break the law by false representation? Closer to the present, how had the man ensured that the palpably innocent Wodd would act as his unwitting accomplice?

A photograph was a photograph: it either reproduced the image of its purported subject or of some other subject. The Vicar on his own admission had signed the backs of Rees's photographs acknowledging that the pictures on the other side were Rees. Simple forgery would have been much less complicated: it would not have been difficult to copy Wodd's signature.

Of course the authorities were more careful about checking passport documentation these days. But here was a case where a respectable parish priest would have confirmed the probity of the matter at least in response to a telephoned or mailed enquiry from the Passport Office.

The question remained: how had the Vicar been duped?

'Has Henry shown you his three card trick?' the Reverend Handel Wodd was making conversation as he replaced the Register in the safe. 'He's not very good at it. Even so, he sometimes foxes me.'

CHAPTER 16

That a Mini Moke was the only motor transport owned
by Henry Nott-Herbert was proof of an eccentricity
Treasure came to accept with good grace—even enthusiasm.

In explaining the matter the evening before, the Judge
had emphasized that since he rarely ventured beyond
walking distance from his home in summer and, if he
could help it, never at all in winter the choice of vehicle
was almost immaterial, except in regard to Devalera.

Mrs Evans, the only other person to be considered, had
long since resigned herself to going everywhere on foot,
bicycle or by bus. She had failed the driving test sixteen
times. In the process she had made a number of enduring
friendships among the Ministry Examiners, but had
eventually given up the contest after backing a car over
a tortoise when both were almost stationary. The tortoise
had escaped unharmed, but Mrs Evans had regarded the
event as a sign.

The Judge's previous car had been a Mulliner-Park
Ward Special Open Tourer Bentley to which he had been
closely attached for all of forty years. After his wife's
death, however, he had sold it to an enthusiast for many
times the sum he had paid for it in the first place. The
transaction suited all concerned save Devalera, who having spent his formative years in the back seat of an open
Bentley was seriously discommoded. It was the car, moving or still, hood up or down, in which Devalera could
arrange to see out without contortion or discomfort.

The dog, like his master, rarely motored anywhere so
that the loss of the Bentley hardly upset his travelling
arrangements. Much more to the point, the back seat of

the Mulliner-Park Ward Special had become Devalera's surrogate mother when he was ten weeks old, and his preferred environment when he came of age. Its womblike soft leather upholstery had enfolded and protected him through the hundred-mile journey from the kennels where he was born to his new home in Panty. Its capaciousness allowed for comfortable growth long after he had abandoned its variety of knobs and tassels as putative sources of suckle. It had become his recognized 'basket' since at the age of around six months he had proved consistently he could vault into it without effort, damage or anything so consequential as the need for a door to be opened—a singular advantage found only in the combination of open car and determined large dog.

Happily the Mini Moke had, as it were, caught Devalera on the rebound. While the Judge had been examining a modest saloon car to replace the Bentley in the showroom of the local garage, his canine companion had quietly settled himself in the rear of the Moke which had been standing forlorn and unsaleable on the forecourt. It hardly matched the opulence of the old love, but for ease of access it beat a Ford Cortina hands down or, more precisely, windows up and roof fixed.

The Judge had bought the little vehicle for his dog, much to the relief of the garage proprietor who, having traded it in nearly new from a sadly disenchanted fine weather motorist, had been despairing about the possibility of ever meeting another who wasn't. The rear seats had been replaced with wheel-to-wheel foam mattressing tastefully covered by Mrs Evans. The collapsible hood had been firmly battened down, and Devalera had taken up residence.

It was understandable, in the circumstances, that where the Moke went Devalera went too, which was why Treasure had been obliged to drive both to the Sunfun Hotel.

The banker had set off conscious that the topless, side-less vehicle with the oversized Irish wolfhound sitting bolt upright in the back needed only a few yards of bunting to qualify as a miniature float in a St Patrick's Day Parade. The short journey completed, however, he had quite warmed to the experience. Devalera showed his affection for the Moke or his disdain for brash hotels—or both—by firmly refusing to leave the one to approach the other.

'Mark, I'm so glad you came.' Patience Crabthorne was standing on the hotel steps, crisp and cool in a blue silk shirt, white pleated skirt and matching broad brimmed hat and shoes.

'Mrs Evans brought your message hot-foot to the churchyard.' Treasure smiled. 'May I say how charming and elegant you look.'

'Thank you, kind sir. It's all the competition around here. Keeps us older girls on our toes.' She smoothed the expensive shirt. 'Money talks, of course, but hell I wish it spoke up louder at my age. Did I fetch you from your devotions?'

'The Vicar and I were discussing card tricks. Actually you saved me from a dress rehearsal of Henry's act, now postponed till eleven-thirty. Where's Edgar?'

'If we walk round the hotel and through the quaintly unestablished garden there's the most spectacular cliff view you ever saw.' She avoided answering the question until they were strolling across a sward of grass punc-tuated here and there by young trees evidently dependent on massive supporting stakes for survival through the windier months. 'I guess they'll try heather and shrubs next year.' They both regarded a willow already nearly denuded of its new yellow foliage by the gusts of May. 'Edgar and Mr Crutt left early in that ludicrous white rac-ing car for a round trip to Llanelli before lunch. They beat the lap record to the hotel gate.'

'They've gone to see the plant?'

'No. The drug factoring outfit—pharmaceutical wholesalers I think you call it over here. Seems it makes a goodly contribution to the pot.'

'Not spectacular but adequate,' Treasure replied absently, wondering what made a closed wholesale warehouse such compulsive viewing on a Bank Holiday Saturday.

'I think they needed to be alone.' Mrs Crabthorne was answering the unspoken question. 'And Mr Crutt feels more comfortable on his own ground. His . . . er . . . his lovely bride is still in bed, where I imagine she spends a good deal of her time,' she added archly. 'Which reminds me, Edgar has given Mr Crutt a fat five-year contract just to run this—what did you say?—not spectacular but adequate factoring subsidiary.'

'When? Do you know?'

'Last night over a nightcap. I heard about it briefly at breakfast. Edgar seems to think that part of the business can be marvellously extended. Do you?' The question came quite sharply and unexpectedly.

'As a matter of fact I don't. Strictly it's not my province to say so. Corporate funding is our—'

'Mark, you're being stuffy.' He returned a look of good-humoured protest. 'That man is useless. Edgar said so two years ago after he'd had him flown around all our plants.'

'That was when your husband was trying to arrange product licensing agreements? Before he decided to buy Rigley & Herbert? I'd forgotten Crutt had been rubber-necked around the kingdom of Hutstacker. Did he go to the Florida plant, d'you know?'

'I expect so. Does it matter?' The question became rhetorical as Patience continued. 'Now isn't that just spectacular?'

They were standing on the cliff path separated by a slim wooden rail from a nearly sheer, two-hundred-foot

drop on to the sea-washed rocky crags and boulders of a
cove due west of Panty. Even on this nearly windless day
the high tide was siphoning spectacularly through the
rocks. It sent spurts of sea and foam by hollows and
crevices to climb and search the lower cliff face before
falling back enfeebled as the roar of the tempest gave way
again to the shrieks of the sea-birds swooping and gliding
over the ever-changing surface of the green, effervescent
water.

'Would you know, the guide says it's nearly inaccessible? I think it's strictly homicidal.' Patience gave a droll
smile. 'I wouldn't count on this handrail—more of an
awful warning than a ready help in trouble. There's an
Iron Age Promontory Fort on the headland over there.'
She pointed to the right. 'And on the other side of that
there's Caerfai beach. That's sandy and fun if you have
the strength to climb the steps up and down.'

'What a lot you get from your guide books.'

'Guide books phooey, I've been tramping this ground
since seven this morning. Edgar's no good on cliff paths,
they give him vertigo. Even some of the pot-holes on Fifth
Avenue give Edgar vertigo. But you were up early too.
Did you solve that mystery you were telling me about?'

'Oddly enough I did.' Devalera could hardly be
credited for his key part in the operation without
awkward explanation. 'Confidentially, it was a misunderstanding.' He hesitated also to mention the subject of the
drowned man, although . . .

'Which frees you to deduce why Edgar has taken such a
shine all of a sudden to the miserable Albert Crutt.' She
was not ready to concede that her husband's new-found
faith in the Managing Director of Rigley & Herbert was
even partially due to his mild engagement with the attrac-
tions of Mrs Crutt. That was simply not Edgar's way.

Thinking about retaining a man because of his attractive wife was quite different from acting on such an

impulse. If Patience had not made a long and deep study of her husband's curious amatory inclinations she would certainly not have put a question that could have prompted Treasure to make a short and shallow enquiry in the same area. More particularly she was a stern public defender of Edgar's moral reputation: that was her way.

'D'you think the liking has been that sudden?' They were now walking back slowly towards the hotel. Privately it went through his mind that Edgar might have been captivated by the curvaceous Bronwen — a preposterous notion which to his credit he dismissed. In any case, he could hardly have put it to Patience.

'Edgar's considered judgement of people is completely reliable. His considered judgement of Mr Crutt as of dinner-time yesterday put him in the shoe clerk category. By breakfast he's practically become one of the family.'

'Running the wholesale company as it stands is a step down from controlling the whole Rigley & Herbert show, of course.'

'The manufacturing part of which is being closed or re-located so there's nothing else to run here except the wholesale company.' Patience had stopped to look again at the wilting willow.

'Probably it's an act of compassion on Edgar's part to keep Crutt on at a modest cost until retirement.'

'Correction. When my husband says a substantial five-year contract, he's not talking about a modest cost. And where business is concerned Edgar has no compassion. Oh, he doesn't throw people out to starve but he never creates jobs for lame brains and he doesn't keep people on in responsible posts whose performances don't shape up.' She turned to face Treasure. 'The only thing Edgar is passionate about right now, passionate enough to account for an uncharacteristic action, is the take-over of Rigley & Herbert.'

'He feels that strongly?' Not for the first time the

banker wondered at the commercial involvement and acuity of so many American wives. 'Then I suppose we deduce something happened last evening that Edgar thought put the deal in peril, something that could be scotched with good old Albert Crutt still on the team.' He paused, pleased with this touch of American idiom. 'And Edgar didn't indicate to you what it could be?'

Patience shook her head. 'Which means it's something he's finding uncomfortable to live with.'

'If that's the case I hardly think I can—'

'Can put your finger on what's bugging Edgar and then stop him using bad judgement? I think you can. He respects you enormously—especially your integrity.'

Treasure doubted he exerted nearly the influence that Patience was suggesting. Earlier he had protested that he had no responsibility for the internal organization of the merged Hutstacker and Rigley & Herbert companies. In theory this was true, but with the acquisition still not quite concluded he had been mildly surprised that Crabthorne had not troubled to take his view on this matter of Crutt.

Most particularly he was still irritated over Crutt's hamfisted and transparent ruse in bringing Crabthorne to Panty in the first place. Since Crabthorne himself had seen through this failed wrecking device, it was fairly evident that the five-year contract was a desperate measure to meet some new desperate and—as Patience suspected—not wholly creditable situation. The last qualification could, of course, be the very reason why Crabthorne had avoided involving his high-principled banker. Treasure debated whether he should be flattered by the reputation or pained by the exclusion.

One point was obvious: Crabthorne and Crutt had not gone to Llanelli to inspect the premises of Rigley & Herbert. They had gone to see Crutt's lawyer who no doubt lived there or nearby and who for friendly or pecuniary considerations would be ready to sacrifice part of a national holiday to draft a letter of intent covering that contract. Treasure was familiar enough with the alarms and excursions that could attend the last stages of a take-over to scent a trail that led hot-foot to lawyers. Crutt might lack panache but he wouldn't be slow to follow up an advantage.

Nor was the banker short of a hypothesis that could explain Crabthorne's sensitive dilemma. On the contrary, it involved a disturbing theory he had been nurturing without enthusiasm and with a growing sense of anxiety for some hours.

'Sorry to keep you waiting.' Treasure rejoined Patience Crabthorne at a table on the hotel's upper terrace. The lower one was entirely occupied by happy, chattering Japanese either consuming breakfast, bowing greetings to those arriving to do so, or bowing farewells to those who had already done so, not counting the few who were doing none of these things because they were photographing all the others who were.

The banker had needed to make a telephone call as well as some enquiries at the reception desk. 'Would you like coffee?' She shook her head in refusal. 'Is it this afternoon you've decided to leave?'

'No. Later on we're looking at the local castles after seeing the Judge's garden, then we head for North Wales early tomorrow. Edgar figured we might outstay our welcome if we hang on any longer. I guess it was a mistake coming at all.'

They exchanged understanding glances, while Treasure remembered his promise to Anna. 'I think Crutt sadly misled Edgar. Anyway the plan sounds admirable. North Wales is very viewable with a whole string of genuine thirteenth-century castles.' He hesitated for a moment before deciding to continue. 'Patience, will you come to Haverfordwest with me now to see something? I'd like to say it's the church there but it's something far less edifying. It could be important though, and it's not far.'

'How intriguing, and of course I'll come. Am I not to know what we're seeing? — Oh, and can we go in your buggy, not my limousine? Just wait till I get a scarf, not that it really matters so long as I'm back here for my hair appointment at eleven.'

So it was that half an hour later Devalera was to be found ready to defend his moveable home in the car park of the Withybush Hospital which lies a mile beyond Haverfordwest on the Fishguard road.

CHAPTER 17

Anna Spring had been out when Treasure called and he
was surprised to find the gallery closed. He had scribbled
a message on a card and pushed it through the letter-box.

He had better luck with his next quarry, Dai Rees the
postman. After dropping a perplexed and thoughtful
Patience Crabthorne back at the hotel in good time for
her hair appointment, he had noticed Dai in the churchyard as he had been driving the Mini Moke in to New
Hall.

'I thought you were the choirmaster not the head
gardener, Mr Rees.'

Dai latched the door of an inconspicuous toolshed that
stood along the north wall of the church. He was holding
a pair of edge-clippers. 'There's three of us give a bit of
time Saturday mornings. I'm finished my own work by
now and every little helps.'

Treasure couldn't help thinking of those twelve thousand bodies. It was small wonder graveyards generated
such abundant greenery though he now considered the
fact in a new light. 'A labour of love, Mr Rees. The Vicar
was singing your praises when he showed me the church
earlier.'

The postman gave a broad grin. 'Saying them anyway.
He's tone deaf. Funny for a Welshman *and* with the
Christian name of Handel.' His expression changed to
one of concern. 'Hear you were still down the harbour
when that body was brought in. There's terrible. First one
this season. Not local, Mr Lewin says. Nasty for you,
though.'

'It was a bit. Violent death too. Not a pretty sight.' He
risked taking the slender opportunity offered. 'Mr Wodd

told me you're an active pacifist. It's not a word one hears much these days.'

The other man chuckled. 'Very behind the times we are down here, Mr Treasure. Yes, I'm a pacifist. My Dad was too—drove an ambulance all through the last war and got blown up more times than most. Suppose I'd do the same if the need came.'

'D'you get involved with anti-nuclear demos?'

'Not in my line, and I wonder if they do much good. No, it's more personal with me. Helping people like me who won't bear arms for conscientious reasons.'

'Not in this country. I mean we don't have conscription . . .'

'No, but in others. Mind you, people think you're cracked bothering these days when there's so much else wrong with the world. For me, though, being made to carry a gun . . . well, I just couldn't do it.'

'And you've a fellow feeling for others with the same loathing without the same liberty.'

'Exactly, Mr Treasure. Take deserters. There's a dirty word for you.' He shook his head. 'There are still unpardoned deserters, thousands of them, in so-called civilized countries whose only crime is one of conscience. Their cause can be helped. People in this village help deserters in many countries.'

'Bit difficult to organize, I should have thought.'

'That's right. Not like your big national causes. More personal—individual, that's the word.'

'Petitions and . . . ?' Treasure, eyebrows raised, waited for further enlightenment.

'Yes, and money for legal fees . . . oh, and other things. If you'd like to know more, Mr Treasure, I can send you . . .'

'To be honest, I'm weighed down with good causes already,' the banker said apologetically, adding as though as an afterthought. 'Does Mrs Spring help?'

'Power of strength—even from the days when she was

here before, as a young girl. Not so active then but keenly
interested.'

'And she remembered your crusading efforts when she
came back.'

'Got involved in similar work in America. There's help
needed there still.'

Treasure was not prepared to argue the point but he
was fairly certain that amnesties had been provided for
US servicemen who had deserted for reasons of conscience
from Vietnam and earlier wars. He looked at his watch. 'I
mustn't interrupt you any longer, Mr Rees.' He was hoping there might be a message from Anna waiting for him
at New Hall.

'Welsh-cakes we call them. Bake-stones some people say.
Nice, aren't they?' Mrs Evans gazed approvingly at
Treasure who, in defiance of his dietary rules, was seated
at her big, scrubbed kitchen table consuming coffee and
a second of the flat, rounded, curranty delicacies with the
powdered sugar coating.

Treasure had found his way to the kitchen a few
minutes earlier in search of information not refreshment.
There he had come upon the housekeeper stacking pyra-
mids of freshly made Welsh-cakes in readiness for the
afternoon. There had been no message for him and he
had been reliably informed that Henry Nott-Herbert,
having locked himself in his bathroom for the purpose of
'serious rehearsal', would be unlikely to appear before he
was scheduled to meet Trteasure at 11.30 unless especially
summoned.

It was the banker's adamant refusal to have a man bid-
den from the hallowed privacy of his own bathroom—
whatever he might be doing there—that had created the
hiatus for 'elevenses'.

'I've spoken to Ethel Ogmore-Davies.' Mrs Evans
delivered this intelligence with a conspiratorial overtone.

'Marvellous what you've done for her peace of mind, and that's a fact.'

'She's told you . . . ?'

'Nothing except what can be officially released.' There followed a knowing nod. 'It'll make things easier for Anna, too. Have another Welsh-cake, Mr Treasure.'

'I don't understand?' He was also trying hard not to yield to proffered further indulgence.

'Well, p'raps I shouldn't say, except His Honour asked you down just to look into Ethel's terrible fright. There's been atmosphere since the engagement. I'll say no more than that. Atmosphere.' More nods. 'But His Honour putting himself out . . . well, it makes for good-will all round.'

If it had not been for a mouth full of Welsh-cake Treasure might have been prompted mildly to protest that the only person remotely inconvenienced so far had been himself. After a moment or two more of pleasurable gluttony he was content with: 'Mrs Ogmore-Davies has something against Mrs Spring marrying the Judge? I thought it was through the Ogmore-Davieses that the two met.'

'Years ago, yes, when Mrs Nott-Herbert was alive. Ethel thinks His Honour's, well . . . far too old for Anna.' There had been a degree of uncertainty—even lack of conviction—in the last comment. 'Then there's Nye, of course. Nye and me. Nothing to do with her really though, as I'm always telling her.'

'You mean she thinks Mrs Spring's marriage to the Judge will affect any . . . er . . . any expectation you and your grandson might entertain . . .'

'When His Honour passes on. That's about it, Mr Treasure, but there's no foundation. I happen to know His Honour's made provision for us out of kindness because he's told me. But there's no obligation. He's not Nye's father or anything like that.'

'Good heavens! Has it ever been suggested he might be?' Treasure was so dumbfounded he had blurted out the question without thinking—an uncharacteristic response which he immediately regretted.

'Not in so many words, and it's all the fault of my Doreen for not saying.'

'Not saying what?' There was no avoiding following through in the belief that the outcome would be less indelicate than the hang-fire implication.

'Who the father was. Wild horses wouldn't drag it out of her. She was of age too, so what could I do?'

Treasure accepted that a stampede of demented stallions might not have forced the tight-lipped Doreen to tell all. 'But you tried to establish who it wasn't?' he demanded. To extend the metaphor, one trained donkey could surely have elicited the fact of the Judge's non-complicity.

Mrs Evans had deserted the Welsh-cakes and, as at breakfast, had taken up her preferred position standing beside her seated, captured-by-comestibles audience. 'Wouldn't utter about it. Still won't. She was living here at the time but working as barmaid in local hotels. His Honour and Mrs Nott-Herbert were ever so good. Insisted she stayed on after the baby was born. That was why the gossips put two and two together and made sixteen and a half. Case of drat-the-senior . . . Employer's rights, like.' Treasure was grateful for the loose translation. Clearly it was from his grandmother that Nye inherited his predisposition toward phonetic approximations. 'Ethel wasn't one of the tarrytiddlers, but when I told her about His Honour's will, after he'd said . . .'

'You told her he was providing for you and Nye?'

'That's right. Well, she did imply.' There was a meaningful pause. 'Not spiteful, mark you . . .' another pause . . .' more like suggesting His Honour was only doing what was proper. We had words, I can tell you . . .

at the time, that was. Over now, of course.' Mrs Evans leant forward a fraction, dropping her voice. 'More to it, though. You see, it was well known the Captain had an eye for the girls, my Doreen being one.'

'You mean it was suggested *he* might have been Nye's father?'

'More than once, I'm sorry to say.'

'So the idea of the Judge . . . ?'

'Very convenient for Ethel. Trouble is, Nye's the spitting image of the Captain. Which could be through family connections,' Mrs Evans added enigmatically. 'Who's to know except my Doreen, and sometimes I wonder if she does. She was going through a very permitted stage at the time.'

With evidently an advertised bent for older men, Treasure thought. 'But now she's happily married,' he said aloud.

'So you can see why Ethel's not keen on Anna marrying His Honour in case it affects Nye's expectancies. She wouldn't admit it, but that's what's behind it.' Mrs Evans was clearly disinclined to change the subject. 'Then there's that old business of Anna and the Captain — not to speak ill of the dead,' which she was now doing, 'but it came up again when he fell to his death outside Anna's front door. Well, nearly. Although Mr Lewin bore witness it was an accident.'

Minutes earlier Treasure had determined to end this slanderous narration — fascinating as it had proved: now he changed his mind. 'Surely Anna was a family friend of the Ogmore-Davieses? I believe she came to help in the house.'

'Well, there were nasty rumours after she'd left that the Captain had been sweet on her all along. Very upsetting for Ethel, true or untrue. Then when Anna came back . . .'

'I thought she'd been welcomed by all and sundry.'

'By most, yes, and even Ethel was sorry for her. But

there's no great love lost between those two, appearances not always being what they seem.'

Mrs Ogmore-Davies's question about whether her husband had fallen or been pushed was still fresh in Treasure's mind. 'I can see it must have been especially difficult, his having died outside Anna's house.'

'Compromising it could have been, Mr Treasure. Who was to know what had happened if Mr Lewin hadn't been passing on his beat within seconds.'

'He saw the Captain fall?'

'Not exactly but nearly. And near enough to know there wasn't anyone else involved. Mark you, Ethel blames Mr Lewin for starting the rumour the Captain was drunk and incapable.'

'Which wasn't mentioned at the inquest.'

'Quite right too, Better that, though, than the accusation he always went home that way hoping to force his attentions on Anna.'

'Who would say such a thing?'

'Between you and me'—and Treasure sincerely hoped this and the rest of the conversation would remain exactly that since he had no desire to figure as a party to an action for defamation—'between you and me,' Mrs Evans repeated even more *sotto voce*, 'Mrs Pugh from the Boatman for one. It's terrible what people will pass on.' She sighed despairingly.

'I consider the humour of Laurel and Hardy must have been mostly visual.' The Judge was sitting on a sofa in Treasure's room. He gazed without enthusiasm at the ventriloquist's dummy which he was balancing on one knee. 'Anyway, I think it's going to rain which means no one will come. If they do I'll manage with card tricks in the big greenhouse.'

Treasure remembered the coloured pasteboard: he had left it on the tall-boy the night before. 'I hope this wasn't part of an important trick. I rescued it from Devalera yesterday. He's chewed one end.' He handed it to Nott-Herbert. 'It's a double-sided card.'

'No, it isn't. It's two cards stuck together with evaporating glue. Just feels like one card. Comes apart at the magician's command. Presto!' What the Judge had in his hand appeared still to be one double-sided card. The volatile adhesive had acquired enduring properties. 'I expect Devalera's ruined it. Actually, it's the magician's aide who's supposed to do the unsticking.'

'The conjuror's proverbially pretty assistant?'

'Beg your pardon? Oh. Magician not conjuror. Professor Popov, you know. Nomenclature. Yes, it ought to be Anna but she's doing the gate today. I've had to recruit the Vicar. He's no good at card tricks,' which seemed to place him in good company, 'so he's doing voices off. Not singing voices . . .'

'Because he's tone deaf.'

'How very perceptive of you, my dear Mark. Now why is it I wanted to see you? Ah, the dress rehearsal. Well we'll scrap that. May not be necessary to have a performance.' He paused for thought. 'I know, Mrs Evans said you had news about . . .'

'About Mrs Ogmore-Davies's body.'

'Good God! It wasn't her they fished out this morning . . . ? No, of course not, you mean her Easter Saturday body.'

'It was all a mistake.'

'Thought as much. And you've sorted it out? Good man. Tell me . . .'

Treasure told the Judge as little as possible and was mildly surprised not to be pressed for more. What pleased the older man was Mrs Ogmore-Davies's solemn undertaking not to raise the matter ever again. 'Of course I'll speak to Lewin,' he replied to the banker's request. 'Tell him the whole thing was a ghastly error. No names, no

pack drill, as you said. You see, he never reported it
properly in the first place. I happen to know because he
told me. He's looking for promotion—don't blame him,
but he won't get it. Putting in daft reports about non-
existent bodies hardly helps. He called it something
else—suspected accident being investigated, something of
the sort, then dropped it. Mrs Ogmore-Davies would be
furious if she knew.'

'Well, if Lewin promises never to raise or discuss the
matter again that's the end of it.'

'Most grateful, Mark. Anna should be too. Could have
been compromising as she whispered to me during tea
yesterday. Never thought of it myself. Some time before
she promised to marry me, and all that.'

'What was compromising?'

'The daffodil business.' The Judge continued in answer
to Treasure's look of deepening mystification. 'You said
yesterday the police might not have asked enough people
about seeing the body. Anna made a joke of it. Said she
could have been down at the quay for all anyone knew.'

'I remember her saying it.'

'Well, she couldn't have . . . been at the quay, I mean.
And if the police had started to ask *everyone* who was up
and about the village at six-thirty that morning I'd have
had to say I was. Taking Anna flowers. In bed.' The Judge
reddened. 'Perfectly innocent action.'

'She was ill?'

'Not at all. I sometimes get up early. There was a new
picture in Anna's gallery I wanted to look at in morning
light. I have a key to the place. Thought I'd trot down
without disturbing anyone. Picked some daffodils on the
way through the garden.' He seemed to lose the thread of
the narrative.

'To leave for Anna. A pleasing gesture,' Treasure
volunteered encouragingly.

'That's it. Nothing to it really, but not anything you'd

want to explain to some busybody policeman.' He chuckled. 'And certainly not the end of the story. It seems I made a hullabaloo opening Anna's front door. When I went up the stairs to leave the flowers I'd woken her. She came out of her bedroom thinking I might be a burglar. Caused quite a commotion I can tell you.'

'I know,' said Treasure involuntarily before adding hastily, 'I mean, I'm sure you did.'

CHAPTER 18

Mark Treasure owned a modest disposition. He needed no pressing to explain the reason for his unusual, early and continuing success in his chosen profession of banking. He genuinely believed his abilities were overestimated by everyone save himself. This, he would argue, had always provided an enormous spur—a need to try harder in order to justify the faith of other people. Personal achievement has been founded on many less commendable premises.

This is not to say that Treasure would humbly countenance being taken for a fool—or the unwitting tool of someone else's unworthy fabrication. This is why, on balance, he found himself doubly irritated: it was becoming fairly obvious not only that sight unseen he *had* been taken for a fool but also that after introduction he had been duped by flattery. This last was the unkindest cut. 'Flattery is good for you,' said the venerable Rector of St Bride's Church in Fleet Street, 'so long as you don't inhale.' Treasure had been inhaling deeply.

On the commendation of an agreeable, retired bishop he had been charged by a charmingly ingenuous old Judge to exercise his wholly overrated powers of criminal detection. This much was acceptable. That he had actually been charged in the process to attempt exposing the nefarious activities of persons directly or indirectly responsible for encouraging the Judge to appoint him to the task was an insult even to an amateur. It was also a clear enough indication that those same persons had used his advertised employment to discourage others from inviting the continuing interest of an obviously more competent authority—namely the police force.

But worst of all the urbane banker had been applying himself with an extra zeal which, he could not conceal, had stemmed from a need to maintain admiring attentions. Nothing could be so humiliating as the awful realization that those attentions had been not merely frivolous but deeply insidious.

It was enough that unprotected widows, superannuated members of the bar and bench of bishops, postmen, clergy, policemen — at least some policemen — not to mention incautious insurance companies and impersonal government departments could have been deftly manipulated. Merchant bankers reckoned they were made of less malleable stuff — even when submitted to burnishment.

It was clear he could not follow a rational inclination to walk away from the whole business. He had performed the favour he had been summoned to provide, and in the process should have secured the deal which had been his only true commission. But he was in too deep — and into something a good deal more serious than Mrs Ogmore-Davies's awful experience.

Nor was the emotional imperative steeling him to persist to do with matters so trivial as his own bruised *amour propre*, the likelihood of some marriage plans being cancelled and the consequent possibility of Hutstacker having to soldier on without benefit of Rigley & Herbert.

To the exclusion of all other considerations Treasure was voluntarily applying himself to what the Judge had in mind for him from the first. He was investigating a mysterious dead body — a real one — in response to an irresistible compulsion wholly unconnected, he told himself, with an attachment as shallow as it had been predictably inept.

Since Anna's call he had delayed only as long as it took a bewildered but compliant Henry Nott-Herbert to telephone an appropriately influential friend, at Treasure's request, for some privileged information. Once this had been obtained the banker set off on foot for the art gallery half way down the hill and for the light luncheon offered by its owner.

This was the fourth time since early morning that Treasure had found himself in the Panty High Street. At six-thirty it had been relatively deserted: now, at midday, the bumper to bumper crawl of westbound traffic witnessed an urban exodus that scarcely proved the boast of the cogniscenti that West Wales was still largely undiscovered.

The trailers and caravans, the tents, inflatable dinghies and household utensils stacked on car roofs, the white faces of the travellers contrasting with the dark of the now heavily threatening rain clouds evidenced that the gipsy in the soul of many an Englishman was still finding outlet—if not at the loss-making Sunfun Hotel.

Many appreciative glances were beaming from traffic-jammed conveyances at the mostly bogus old-world shop fronts along the High Street. It was television advertising come to life: you could almost hear the wrapped brown bread and processed cheese being lovingly compounded in stone-flagged kitchens ready to be rumbled away in hand carts up country lanes to heaven knows where to the accompaniment of better known bits from the Pastoral Symphony.

'Thank you for inviting me.' Treasure embellished the greeting with the looked-for formal kiss upon the cheek. Why did this make him feel like a Judas, he wondered— perhaps because Anna was innocent until proved otherwise. He wished they could dispense with the preliminaries.

'It makes it easier for Mrs Evans today with the garden refreshments to arrange. Henry doesn't take lunch anyway. You said on your note you wanted a private word.'

Anna locked the street door after he had entered,

hanging a 'Closed' sign in the centre glass panel. Then she turned to face her visitor.

'So?' She leaned back against the door, arms limp at her side, chin high, eyes wide open and questioning. 'You'd like to see the pictures?'

He shook his head. 'Later perhaps.' She hadn't moved. Was she willing him to reach out for her?

'There isn't much to see right now. Local artists' work. Quite nice and inexpensive for holidaymakers. Now they begin to arrive. You saw the traffic in the street?'

'Henry has all your best stuff I expect.' He paused. 'Anna, I have—'

'Last night I embarrassed you.' She interrupted deliberately. 'You feel compromised over your wife, or Henry, or both of them perhaps.'

'Not at all.'

She smiled. 'Guilty then, and that's worse for an Englishman. It's my fault. I am of course indiscreet and perhaps I have spoiled our friendship before it properly started. There. Now you can scold me. Say it's shameless of me to be impulsive—to take what I want . . .'

'Wrong again. I thoroughly enjoyed last evening. Every moment.' Which probably suggested she hadn't been impulsive enough: this was not what he had come to say. He started again. 'I want to help you.'

'Help?' She stared straight into his eyes: now there was a touch of mockery in the expression.

'Don't misunderstand, Anna. I'm here to talk to you seriously . . . about your husband. Could we . . . ?'

She held his gaze for a split second longer, then, pushing herself away from the door, she brushed past him without hesitation and made for the spiral staircase in the centre of the gallery. 'I promised you a drink before lunch,' she called.

He followed, determined that neither the scent of her nor the sight of that tightly clad form lithely climbing the

steps ahead of him nor anything else about this bewitch-
ing woman would deter him from following the course he
had embarked on.

He had not noticed her smoking before. Now she was
lighting the fourth of the long, brown-papered cigarettes
she had taken up in the twenty minutes they had been
together. The three others she had discarded, half smoked,
in the big glass ashtray. They both held drinks in their
hands: Anna had hardly touched hers. Only the cigarettes
belied her composure.

'And assuming this hypothetical situation that I know
my husband is alive, it would make a difference if I could
prove I first believed him to be dead. That I was not a
conspirator?'

They were sitting across from each other on black
leather sofas set at right angles to the large picture window that had replaced the south wall of the upper floor:
the window opened on to a narrow wrought-iron balcony.
The gallery extended to the front half of the higher
storey. Anna's private apartment was partitioned off near
the top of the stairs.

The main room was bigger than Treasure had expected—low-ceilinged with white walls contrasting with
the gauds of bright colours in the pictures, the scatter
rugs and the furnishings generally. A closed door on one
side of the room presumably let onto the sleeping and
bathroom arrangements while an open one opposite
revealed a well-equipped kitchen.

'I'm not a lawyer, and I'm not a policeman.' Treasure
wanted to add he regretted he was also not a smoker: it
was six months since he had given up the pipe he would
dearly liked to have been fingering since the interview
began, and most particularly since Anna had taken consolation in those cigarettes. 'I believe there must be a
distinction between conspiring to defraud before the

event and being—what shall we say?—more or less obliged to co-operate afterwards.' He paused. 'Anna, I've told you I want to help you. I wish we could stop fencing about hypotheticals. It's all supposition on my part, but a lot of it's provable for the asking.' She remained silent. 'I came down in the train yesterday with your husband who was assaulted and then carried off or else he ran away of his own accord. I suspect the latter.

'I saw him again outside the Cathedral last evening. I believe it was your husband because I believe he was recognized by at least one of the Crabthornes and very possibly by two other people. No one has spoken out yet—of their own accord. No doubt they have their reasons. I can't believe they'll be permanent ones.'

He was not yet ready to admit to Anna the circumstances in which he had obtained a near definite if unvolunteered identification of Ralph Spring.

'So the husband you claim perished in an air accident somehow survived and came to Britain. He may not have had your help getting here, but he's had it since. For instance, you got him a passport, I think, by pretending to Dai Rees he was an American deserter friend. Dai actually applied for a passport in his own name but with your husband's picture on it. The Vicar authenticated the photographs which Dai had stuck on the backs of pictures of himself. With thin prints and volatile glue—the sort Henry uses—Wodd wouldn't have suspected anything. You didn't have to sweet-talk the Vicar too.' There was no bitterness in his tone. 'Dai described himself as a clerk. Postal clerk? Postman? Acceptable enough to all concerned I suppose.'

Anna's eyebrows rose a fraction in response, but she still said nothing.

'If this whole thing was a conspiracy from the start, then it's easier to guess the scenario, although, if it can be proved, the consequences will be more serious for you.

After establishing your husband's death and collecting on
the insurance, you planned to come together again in
Panty, eventually. There'd be some risk, but it's pretty
out of the way down here. First, though, you meant to
talk Henry into befriending you—even perhaps marrying
you. You knew he was fond of you, that his wife was dead
and through . . . er . . . a relationship with Edgar Crabthorne you knew that Hutstacker's could possibly be on
the way to making Henry very, very rich. And the scheme
worked. Your husband was happy to keep his distance—
though I think he visited you here at least once.'

Treasure got up, walked to the drinks table and
replenished his glass with ice and soda but not more
whisky. He glanced enquiringly at Anna's drink: it was
still almost untouched. He was in time to light her fifth
cigarette for her before he sat down again. She nodded
her thanks without looking up at him.

'The gallery was the perfect way to bring Henry seriously
into your life and even if it kept your husband out it introduced Detective-Inspector Iffley who, I suspect, to use your
own phraseology, you reached out for impulsively—and
took.

'I know a bit about Iffley's work because he told me. I
think it probable your relationship with him makes for
profit and pleasure. He's engaged in a perfectly legit-
imate way with the overlaps of highly illegitimate traders.
He's after drugs, but in the process it may be politic for
him to buy lesser known but still valuable works of art
coming on the market by devious means. Has he also been
going out of his way to do so? "Anna's finds" Henry calls
them. They're frankly so superior to anything you have
here I'm surprised even Henry hasn't queried their origins
more carefully, particularly since he's providing the
seller's good title.

'Did Iffley spoil your relationship with your husband?
Something did. Something brought Mr Spring here

yesterday in the face of a good deal of opposition. Who laid that on I wonder? Could it have been the Inspector? He was very conveniently placed when those under-nourished desperados on the train needed lifting out. They thought they had a car meeting them. Instead it may have met me.

'Iffley drove me here, but he didn't exactly hang around Panty afterwards. Risked being seen here too often, perhaps?' He nodded towards the balcony. 'Easter Saturday must have been a close thing with Henry standing here with his daffodils and Iffley climbing down the wrought-iron—naked and practically into the arms of Mrs Ogmore-Davies.'

Anna looked up at this, but still she didn't speak.

'Which brings us back to your husband. Ralph, isn't it? If I'm half right about what's been going on, Ralph would have plenty of reason to feel cut out of things—perhaps even his share of the insurance money, not to mention a loving wife. And a supposedly dead man has so few rights when you think about it. But having failed to get what he wants by 'phone or previous visits he came yesterday, set-ting out, at least, disguised as a clergyman. An Australian clergyman. Somebody knew he was coming but the at-tempt to waylay him—or whatever it was—didn't work.

'What upset everything, of course, was not the expected arrival of Ralph but the unexpected one of the Crabthornes and Albert Crutt. They all know him by sight. Altogether he picked a bad day and I'm surprised someone didn't warn him in his own interests to go away or get disguised again. Was there a rendezvous at the cathedral?'

He paused only momentarily watching the huge rain-drops that had begun to fall on the balcony. 'And were you scared I might see that wedding photo, the one that mysteriously disappeared from the Ogmore-Davies ditty box, the one you'd forgotten you'd sent her? It was clever to go back for it. I suppose you have a key to Mariner's Rest. It's curious I don't remember Mrs Ogmore-Davies talking about the picture when you were there. I hadn't asked to see it. I might have today.'

It was as though he was talking to himself. There was no visible reaction from Anna yet he was conscious this was the cruellest soliloquy he had ever felt obliged to deliver—even so, and paradoxically, he hoped fervently that for Anna the worst was still to come.

'Whether I'm right or wrong on some of the detail I know I'm right on the central facts about Ralph. I can't guess yet how much trouble you're in. You must decide how much you want to tell me, if you want my help or if you feel the whole thing is none of my business.' So this was it. 'Up to this morning you seem to have been involved in nothing more terrible than an insurance swindle and in the obtaining of a false passport. But a few hours ago your husband was taken out of the sea. He was dead. There's no question about identity. I give you my word, it was he.'

The following silence he found almost unendurable.

'He drowned himself.' She said at last—slowly and deliberately, not as a question but as a statement. They were the words he had wanted to hear.

'I'm sorry, but there appears to be some doubt. He wasn't drowned. It could have been an accident, or suicide, or . . . or murder.'

'Then whatever it was I killed him.' The tears were now coursing down her cheeks. There was no audible sobbing, just the tears and the expression of utter despair. 'I loved him . . . Once upon a time I loved him.'

'And I don't believe you had anything to do with his death.' Treasure was convinced the emotion displayed was genuine. 'Drink your drink, then tell me about it,' he added gently.

CHAPTER 19

Not far away from Anna Spring's living-room a figure had paused to gaze out over St Brides Bay—to gaze and to contemplate

It was, of course, the perfect crime. Granted, you were half way there with Ralph Spring supposed to have copped it over a year ago: made it easier to live with too.

Anna was expecting her husband or his messenger to pick up the money at 3.00. And that was exactly what would seem to happen. So far as she was concerned her husband would be stepping out of her life two hours from now—bitter and resentful but well off, and alive; never to be heard of again.

It would be the messenger who made the pick-up, but so what? Spring had had good reason to be suspicious: why shouldn't he have sent a messenger? The last thing Anna would think about was a double cross.

All the same it would have been a lot safer to have had that body float in a day or two later, or better still a day or two later and miles away. It should have been ditched further up the coast, of course, but time had been critical to the whole operation. Getting the clothes off and the swimming trunks on had taken too long as it was. The thing to avoid was putting signs out for over-keen pathologists.

'The most difficult problem is to separate immediate ante-mortem from immediate post-mortem bruises.' That was in the text-book—it had stuck in the memory. 'The blow from the sandbag can be just as dangerous but so much more diffused and less determinable than one from a blunt instrument. The sandbag is much used in interrogation by totalitarian regimes.'

Well, all that needed establishing was a simple case of over-enthusiastic swimmer falling off rocks, getting bumps on head, and cuts all over, precipitating accidental death: please inform the next of kin.

With luck it could happen that way. With no luck at all and if foul play was suspected, trying to find the motive for an attack on a totally unidentified victim was archive stuff almost before it got on file.

It was a pity about the platinum watch: wasteful and careless. Still, it added credibility to the accident theory: foul players rarely left spoils.

It was even more of a pity that the whole thing had been drawn out into two acts. If it had gone according to plan Spring should have had the bag of money with him last night and by now all would have been safely over.

Still, the rain was a godsend. With all the wet weather gear on you couldn't tell a woman from a man motor-cyclist—and that mattered a good deal.

'They're going to believe I killed him in any case. Ralph left a letter for Scotland Yard.'

Anna turned from the window where she had been standing. Unlike the rain, the tears had stopped. She took the fresh iced drink from Treasure and sat again on the sofa.

'Glyn—that's Inspector Iffley—thought maybe the letter didn't exist, that it would have been too dangerous for Ralph to leave with anyone.'

'Was there any reason he should think he was in danger before . . .'

'Before yesterday on the train? No. Not physical danger.'

'Then with his deep knowledge and understanding of the criminal mind Iffley's probably right,' said Treasure with undisguised acerbity.

'If there is a letter will I be arrested anyway?' There was

now curiously little emotion in the tone of her voice.

'Well, certainly not on suspicion of murder. Assuming it was murder—and that's a very big assumption—at the relevant time you were seen selling pictures, listening to organ music or else you were alone with me'—a fact that would no doubt add colour to any reports in the popular press: but there it was.

'You would say so?'

'Of course I'd say so.' He wished he were as confident about his right to have reported official timings and uncertainties even though Henry had passed them on like the weather report.

'Thank you, Mark,' she said quietly. 'You'll take food from the kitchen? It's all prepared . . .'

Treasure shook his head. 'Not for the moment. I'd rather be listening to your story—from the beginning.'

She rolled the cold glass across her forehead. 'From the beginning the air charter business was a failure. We were broke. Worse, we were getting deeper into debt. From that time, also, our marriage was failing.' She looked up. 'The air accident was a golden opportunity. Ralph took it, and then there was no turning back.

'Oh, the plane crashed—disappeared as I told you, but Ralph wasn't in it. He felt unwell at the last minute and decided to stay over after all. The flight was from a private airstrip. The pilot had got official clearance for Ralph and himself and he'd never altered it. They were both eventually reported killed.

'Ralph had tried to 'phone me but couldn't get through. He spent the night in a rooming-house, heard about the freak storms on the radio—including reports of a Mayday call from an American charter plane with two people in it. He checked anonymously by 'phone later in the day and heard he had been reported missing. There was a search over several days but they found nothing.'

'He didn't try to reach you again?'

'I thought he was dead until he called me three weeks later from Brazil. He begged me to go along with the plan he'd made. And it was so simple. It meant we could collect on the insurance and start again somewhere. No, not here, but somewhere — together. Perhaps to build our marriage again.'

She took a sip from her drink. 'Ralph thought fate or something owed him that much — the airlines because he was passed over for promotion so many times — me because I was sick of life at the level we'd had to lead it. I guess he'd been afraid of losing me . . . now he could . . . he could buy me back.

'Ralph is . . . was not a strong character. He needed me. I don't know whether I ever needed him.' There was a longish pause. He thought the tears might be returning but she swallowed hard and continued evenly. 'When he decided to stay dead he had a hundred thousand American dollars on him — delivery payment on the plane he'd ferried down. He knew there'd be no claim about the money. It was a side deal in cash on the plane — to save the seller some tax. You understand?'

Treasure understood. 'Quite a windfall. And the insurance?'

'Was not so easy or so quick. They finally paid me two hundred and fifty thousand dollars on Ralph's life a few months ago. I guess they needed to be certain.'

As a director of two insurance companies — chairman of one of them — Treasure nodded wistfully. He asked the name of the insurance company. She told him. 'I expect you received an advance to keep you going.'

'That's right. By then I'd been here some time. We arranged that. It wasn't intended Ralph and I settle here. Obviously that would have been too risky. We'd figured to end up in France — in Provence. Here it was credible for me to come for a while. Somewhere I didn't need to build from nothing — where life wasn't a whole lie.'

'And became less and less of a lie, perhaps?' Treasure did not wait for a reply. 'And Henry?'

'Was not as you guessed. Sure I knew he was rich. I knew also about Hutstacker's from Edgar Crabthorne.' For the first time a faint if fleeting smile showed on her face. 'It was a very chaste affair. Edgar likes to talk about his business—but by assignation and candlelight!' She looked down. 'Henry wanted to help. He's dear and sweet. He insisted on lending me the money for the gallery and . . . well . . . we just drifted together in this father-daughter relationship as I thought.'

'Until he asked you to marry him.'

'Which was well after Glyn Iffley had come into my life.' The regret in that sentence was too marked to ignore.

'Meantime your husband?'

Anna sighed. 'Ralph came to England in October from Brazil through Frankfurt, Dublin and, I think, Belfast. That's a route where you don't show your passport, only wave it—provided you stay in transit and have no luggage. He had to risk using his own passport still, until he got to this country when I could arrange the new one. You guessed right about that. Dai Rees was very obliging—and very innocent.

'Ralph had plenty of money and a new identity. I was all right here. We'd figured not to meet for two years, or until we felt it was safe. Ralph was to buy a place in France at the end of this summer . . .' Her voice trailed away.

'So the plan had worked,' Treasure put in, 'except . . .'

'Except I'd fallen out of love with my husband, that I'd become infatuated with Glyn, too involved with Henry . . .'

'And expert in dealing with stolen pictures?'

She shook her head. 'They're not stolen. It's to do with avoiding capital tax. At the start I thought they were genuine discoveries Glyn made doing his cover job as a dealer. Does that sound ingenuous? Probably—but it's true. Later he told me how it works. It's not dishonest. The people who sell the pictures are the real owners but they don't want the sales traced back to them. Of course it's a strictly cash business. I have to keep a lot of money here.'

'Of course,' the banker answered lightly. On any other occasion he would have felt obliged to straighten out the morality just expounded. As it was, he merely savoured in passing the piquant thought that squads of impoverished 'honest' Welsh gentry had been trundling out their lesser-known old masters to exchange for ready cash at the door with a detective-inspector of Police.

Judging by the number of good pictures that appeared to be passing between Anna's gallery and New Hall it seemed Iffley was not relying entirely on the fruits of his own house-calls: no doubt there were established middle-men in the sensitive business of this kind of tax evasion. Certainly the Inspector was well organized—not least in having Anna's funds at his disposal; cash flow and owner-ship problems solved on request by Henry Nott-Herbert.

'Glyn wants to resign from the police.' And who could blame him? 'At one time we planned to run the gallery together, perhaps to marry.' Anna added: 'That was before Henry proposed to me.'

'Iffley was willing to wait in line of course until in due time you became Henry's widow.' Treasure was beginning to dislike Inspector Iffley more and more, so much so he had difficulty stifling the thought that perhaps the man might not be beyond accelerating the demise of Judge Nott-Herbert once he was married to Anna. She had not reacted to his last comment before he asked. 'When did you tell Iffley the truth about your husband?'

'When we became lovers. It would have been imposs-ible otherwise.' These came as straight statements without elaboration. 'Ralph had taken a service apartment in

London. We talked often by telephone. At the beginning of November I told him there was no point in going on. That I had met someone else. That we should go our own ways. He was desolate. He begged to see me. Stupidly I gave in. I agreed he could come here for one night. He hired a car and arrived after dark. No one need have seen him. It's simple to get from a car into this house.'

'There was no street light outside then,' Treasure added absently. 'Did Iffley know he was coming?'

'Yes. He was against it, but he knew. I arranged it for a night he had to be away on police work to avoid . . . a confrontation. Otherwise he might have been here when . . .' She faltered. 'Ralph was ecstatic to be with me. I think also heart-broken that seeing him meant nothing to me. He pleaded . . . begged me to go back to him.' She shook her head. 'It was no good, of course. We were arguing still when the terrible thing happened.'

'To your husband? To Ralph?'

'No. At around eleven-thirty there was an awful crash outside, a cry for help—a hideous shout I shall never forget. We rushed outside—what anyone would do. It was the Captain—Captain Ogmore-Davies.'

Treasure understood. 'It was the night he died.'

'His heart, you understand. He must have grasped for the wall, then fallen down the steps. We had to help—or try to. It was instinctive. The house opposite is empty in winter. There was no one else about . . .'

'Except Constable Lewin,' said Treasure slowly.

'Shortly he came. Too late. We were all too late. The Captain was dead.'

'And Lewin?'

'He heard me call Ralph by his name. I didn't know if he'd realized it was my husband. That night there was nothing to do except have the body taken away. Lewin said he would come next day to take statements. Thank God Glyn Iffley telephoned at one in the morning. I told

him what happened. He said Ralph should leave right
away and that he'd square Lewin first thing. He did.
Lewin was here for over an hour next day, here in this
room taking my statement. Neither of us mentioned
there'd been another . . . another witness.'

'So no one ever knew Ralph was with you?'

Anna nodded. 'And that was the last time I saw him.'

'But Lewin knew he was alive.'

'He guessed after a while but he didn't make trouble.
Glyn promised to help him get promotion. I think he paid
him a little too.' She saw Treasure's eyebrows rise. 'He has
a bad life . . . with his wife. He is not corrupt, I think.
And he has helped me. When you live a lie . . .'

'It helps to have the support of your friendly
neighbourhood policeman.' There was a touch of acidity
in his tone. 'So of course Lewin knew perfectly well who
Mrs Ogmore-Davies saw that morning on the boat.'

Anna coloured. 'Glynn telephoned him later. Yes . . .
I'm sorry.'

'And you knowingly let Henry get me down here on a
wild goose chase thinking there was no chance of my . . .'
He paused. 'Oh well. We'll let that one pass. I'm more
interested in knowing why your husband was here yesterday—and why he chose to travel with me.'

'He chose to be here when you were here. He didn't
mean to travel with you. Maybe he *was* scared . . . of
Glyn.'

'He knew *Inspector* Iffley was the other man. How did
he know I was coming?'

Anna sighed. 'For months he's been telephoning non-
stop. At the beginning he is still trying to make me
change my mind. Then he accepts what is to happen and
he needs to know about the money. Glyn said I should
offer him half. He's not content with that. He wants
three-quarters. He tries to persuade me to go to London
to discuss the split. Glyn is against this. Then Ralph says

he's coming here to talk to both of us without enmity, to make a civilized agreement, and to pick up his share . . .'

In the few minutes more it took Anna to unfold the story Treasure became convinced murder had been done—and he thought he knew by which of the three prime suspects.

Spring had certainly known or sensed he was in danger—before the assault on the train. He had refused to tell Anna on what day he was coming to Panty—only that he would travel incognito and telephone on arrival. He had been warned about Treasure's visit and broadly the purpose of it, yet he had chosen to come at the same time. It had been coincidental the two had travelled in the same compartment but Anna was sure Spring had thought Iffley would be more circumspect with Treasure about.

Iffley had used his authority to have Spring's movements checked each morning in London since the day he had said he was coming to Panty. It had been simple enough to have him under temporary surveillance as a suspected drug-trafficker.

So the Inspector had known on the day how and when Spring was travelling—also how he was disguised. He had told Anna he proposed boarding the train himself at Llanelli for a pre-emptive, man-to-man discussion with her husband. Instead he had sent the two hooligans to get the passport for use as a bargaining device. They were only to threaten violence—at the most to 'rough up' the victim. He denied giving them a gun but he had supplied the British Rail corridor key that should have kept the carriage isolated for the few seconds required for the assailants to do their work and get away.

A variety of contingency plans had been made in case Spring had decided to take lunch on the train, including rifling his unattended luggage and, if necessary, waylaying him between carriages. What had not been allowed for was Treasure's early return from the dining car.

Iffley had been powerless to extricate his fumbling accomplices when they escaped on the wrong side of the station with the level-crossing gates closed to road traffic. Instead he had used the initiative with which Treasure had earlier credited him by appearing on the scene at the same time as the local police. Indeed he had been ahead of them, waiting in a side street to pick up his stooges, but he had delayed a decent interval after hearing the police broadcast.

It had been a simple job for Iffley to succeed where the others had failed: he had palmed the passport himself while officially going through the contents of Spring's case. Observing a two-month-old rule not to dally in Panty, and especially not to approach Anna's house in daylight, he had then carefully taped the passport in the folds of the box, stopped at the first pay-phone beyond St David's, and told Anna to retrieve it—which accounted for her prompt appearance at New Hall.

There had been enough ready cash in Anna's small safe to pay Spring the £100,000: it appeared there was always enough cash in Anna's safe. Nor was she prepared to dispute her husband's right virtually to all the insurance money as well as the return of the passport. Iffley had opposed all this, but to no purpose in the face of what had clearly been Anna's rocklike determination. She had considered the assault inexcusable and Spring's retribution justified. She was in any case tired of Iffley's haggling: in view of her intended marriage to Henry the listener had found this view entirely reasonable.

Anna had also insisted that Spring's over-cautious arrangements at the cathedral should be observed, that she should hand over the money herself, and that Iffley should not be present. It had been her intention to leave the picture-selling to the other helpers and at 8.20 to move to the appointed seat in the back row.

The unheralded arrival of the Crabthornes had of course totally jeopardized the plan. Anna had no way of reaching her husband. Between drinks and dinner at New Hall she had tried to telephone Iffley without success. In desperation she had 'phoned Constable Lewin who she trusted in the hope he might be able to contact Iffley— through police channels!—with a message to join her urgently.

Aware that even the lack-witted Lewin must have sensed drama in her tone, Anna had reasoned there would be no extra risk and possibly great advantage in enlisting his further help—with circumspection. She had asked him as a favour to stand near the cathedral door from 8.15 in the hope he could waylay a clergyman with an Australian accent—description supplied but name unknown—with the news that a number of unexpected American friends were attending the recital: she had no way of knowing that Spring had abandoned disguise.

The Constable had predictably failed in his mission, but had shown no surprise nor questioned the propriety of his being recruited. Perhaps he believed such favours brought promotion nearer.

It had been Treasure, after the recital, who had unknowingly calmed Anna's worst misgivings. Clearly Spring had seen the danger for himself and got away from it—or so Anna believed at the time.

The account of the early telephone call that morning had completed Anna's story. She was sure it had been a woman's voice. Before Treasure had told her Spring was dead she had been prepared to hand over the case with the money and passport at 3 o'clock.

'You were never aware Albert Crutt knew your husband?' Treasure asked. He was standing beside a small desk near the bedroom door. It supported a typewriter, a telephone and a big address book. He was leafing through a section of the book. 'Crutt's never mentioned it to you?'

Anna answered from the kitchen where she was preparing coffee. The two had eaten a little: he more than she. 'I didn't know they'd met. Ralph may have flown him around the plants that time. As for Mr Crutt mentioning it to me: we met for the first time yesterday. Henry never asks him to Panty.'

Treasure glanced up. He was sure he had found the masked entry he wanted—and in about twenty seconds. It was in the crypto-logical place and form he had expected Anna would use: the London exchange was the same as his own.

He walked back to where they had been seated. Anna was placing a coffee tray between them. 'Tell me. You've taken me at my word. I do want to help you—as much as I can. But you've told me more than a lawyer would advise you to tell—particularly about your relationship with Iffley. Why . . . ?'

'Because that relationship is over.' Her voice was even, the delivery slow and considered. Now she stood tall and quite still except for her eyes which were searching his for a reaction. 'Because I believe Glyn Iffley murdered my husband.'

'I'm not sure I agree,' Treasure said gravely, 'but you know, there's only one way we're going to find out.'

CHAPTER 20

'Lucy Cramphorn. Never any good in a draughty bed. Same goes for Wendy Cussons.' Henry Nott-Herbert emitted these promising calumnies as commonplaces. 'Put 'em up against a wall though — either of 'em — marvellous. Perform differently in the Home Counties. Down here they need coddling.'

'Cuddling?' Treasure corrected tentatively.

'If you like,' the other replied. He turned about, leading the banker from the broad south terrace, around the house, to the front drive.

The Judge was sporting a deerstalker hat, belted Norfolk jacket and matching knickerbockers, the ensemble he considered proper for garden openings and which would have served as well for a day out with a genteel Victorian Cycling Club. In truth his appearance was as eccentrically distinguished as he intended it to be distinguishing. This year he was determined not to be mistaken for one of his own gardeners: again. And the hazard was increasing since what had once been an army of outside retainers had latterly been reduced to one Italian, part time, who on these occasions tended to dress and behave like a successful film director.

Henry glanced here and there while continuing his commentary. 'We've got Lady Seton on the side here, spreading nicely.' He nodded vaguely in the direction of the Vicarage. 'No trouble. Extremely free habits and vigorous with it. Very popular in the area. Now let's see if the rain's done anything for Konrad Adenauer.' It seemed to Treasure it would take more than a drop of rain . . . 'Grow roses yourself?' the Judge put in as an afterthought. 'Know about them?'

'Not much but I'm learning.' The Treasures' garden in Cheyne Walk was stone-flagged with a ground area smaller than their kitchen—hardly suitable for Lady Seton. 'We tend to go for herbs,' he added defensively. 'Isn't it early yet for roses?' The price at Moyses Stevens shop in Berkeley Square suggested as much, and that was as close as he usually got to roses in the raw.

'All to do with sun and shelter. Oh, and the right kind of dung. Those are the Adenauers, just inside the gate, with Lady Penzance behind. You're right, though. Even the earlies need another two weeks.'

'Lady Penzance is showing a bit.' This was Treasure keeping his end up but not sedulously. It was 2.15 and he had returned to New Hall ten minutes earlier. The Judge's rosy discourse was claiming only half his attention while he silently pondered on weightier considerations— like Albert Crutt.

Crutt had driven his wife and the Judge to the cathedral ahead of the others last evening. It followed he could have run into Spring before anyone else—or seen him at least.

But had Spring seen Crutt? If he had, wouldn't he have turned tail before Treasure and the Crabthornes had come along?

If Crutt had recognized Spring he had the makings of his five year contract right there. If he threatened to tell the Judge his darling Anna's first husband was alive and visiting, then Anna—along with her advice on Rigley & Herbert—might be very quickly abandoned

But might Crutt have taken even sterner measures enduringly to placate rather than opportunely to coerce his putative new master? He had been a *very* long time parking the car: long enough to have cornered Spring—for discussions about insurance payouts, deals: long enough for the staging of accidents? The chap seemed timorous enough until you remembered his bold if rather fatuous ploy in bringing the Crabthornes to Panty: case of *cherchez la femme* perhaps—and you could hardly miss Bronwen.

It was not conceivable that Crabthorne would condone violence, but then there was no necessity for that. Almost certainly he had seen Spring at the cathedral at the same moment as Treasure. Thereafter Spring would have become a growing hazard until he was assured the danger had somehow but definitely been overcome—the man paid off, threatened with exposure . . . anyway neutralized. One would be careful not to suggest eliminated: it wasn't that type of contract Crutt had been given, unless he had taken it upon himself to . . .

'Wet under foot but the rain's stopped for good.' Nott-Herbert had drawn Treasure towards the gate and had halted to survey the sky and to dig his brogues into the loose gravelled drive like a golfer preparing to play out of a deep bunker. 'Drains off fast enough, but we make 'em park cars in the road. Oh, forgot to tell you. Punch and Judy man's coming. Rang me this morning. Emigrated to Canada. Found it too cold . . . or was it Australia too hot? Anyway, he's back. Doing his show at three. Should be here shortly.'

Iffley's parked car at The Popples: one had to accept it had seemed like the damning inconsistency. That was why Treasure hadn't mentioned it to Anna who was already convinced enough about her lover's treachery. If the man had not known about the Crabthornes, if Anna had failed to reach him, if he had not been available to help head off Spring, if he normally avoided being seen in the area, why had his car been parked where it was? It was arranged that Anna would pass over the money—the payoff Iffley so much resented. Nothing Anna had said implied she knew the policeman had been in St David's, yet they had since talked on the telephone.

'Ought to tell Handel Wodd shan't be needing him

after all. With the Punch and Judy here, best to give my performance a miss, don't you think?' The Judge waited in vain for protest from his preoccupied guest. 'No point gilding the lily,' he added ruefully and more or less to himself.

'I'll tell the Vicar. I'll pop across now,' said Treasure as though on impulse.

Constable Lewin had missed Spring outside the cathedral because he had been looking for a hairy clergyman. Otherwise he might have recognized him even though their first meeting had been brief and in the dark. Spring's abandoning his disguise was, Treasure now considered, so significant as to be the key to the whole puzzle.

The Vicar was emptying the locked offertory box which was encased in a stone pillar at the back of the church — a necessary twice-daily precaution at holiday time, he explained. While there would be more visitors putting money into the box, this apparently increased the incidence of callers whose single unauthorized purpose was to attempt taking it out.

He was pleased to know he was no longer required as ventriloquist's stooge and then readily agreed to perform the function begged by Treasure.

The banker had been loath to involve official authority in his plan. Thus it was gratifying that both the volunteers he had enlisted were providing somewhat curious services without benefit of explanation.

Back in the narrow road outside Constable Lewin was supervising the reversing of a large motor-coach full of eager Japanese. He was also trying to control the movements of a shoal of lesser vehicles while pretending not to hear the abuse being hurled in his direction by the immense and angry driver of a very small van.

'I've come to entertain the frigging kids and they're not going to be out here they're going to be in frigging there. Frigging coppers!' The huge, purple-faced complainant

directed his last sally at Treasure more because he had
moved within earshot than because he looked a likely
source of aid.

'Are you the Punch and Judy man?' Treasure asked
affably. Four double chins moved in grateful affirmation
below signs of fading apoplexy. 'Mr Lewin, I think we
ought to squeeze this gentleman through with his van'—
and assuming it would afterwards be possible to extricate
him from it—'He'll be wanted inside.'

Lewin held up an admonitory hand at the coach
driver, swept an 'I-dare-you' look at the others and
walked over towards the van. As he did so and behind his
back Handel Wodd's middle-aged estate-car slipped
quietly out of the Vicarage gate, just scraped past the rear
of the temporarily arrested coach and disappeared along
the descending farm track beyond.

Half an hour later Treasure had stationed himself in the
New Hall drive where Anna knew he would be, some
yards from the gate. She was sitting behind a table in the
gateway taking entrance money and issuing tickets for
tea. There was a man's briefcase on her lap. The table
was decorated with posters for the Royal National
Lifeboat Institution.

Devalera was unwittingly performing stand-by sentinel
duty. He was asleep in the back of the Mini Moke which
Treasure had purposely left at a handy distance in the
drive. In view of the press of parked cars outside,
however, the possibility of being able to take even the tiny
Moke anywhere seemed fairly remote. Lewin had long
since been obliged to shift his constabulary duties to the
end of the road which, he had explained to Treasure,
normally rated as a cul-de-sac but which at church service
times and for special events easily degenerated into a confusing car park—it seemed even when under supervision.

The steady trickle of garden visitors seemed not to have

diminished in the half-hour since opening time.

Mrs Ogmore-Davies had earlier confided in Treasure that the tea was the attraction—but in a voice loud enough to have brought a delighted blush to the cheeks of Mrs Evans who was standing next to her on the terrace ready to fill cups and dispense confections from the long trestle table.

Both ladies were—somewhat self-consciously—dressed in traditional Welsh costume complete with woven shawls and black stove bonnets. Their garb had no particular relevance to the occasion but had been acquired for a pageant earlier in the year. It had seemed a pity not to give it a second airing. Thus the two were delighting the Japanese almost as much as the photogenic appearance of the Judge in his Sherlock Holmes outfit.

An orderly queue of male Orientals had formed on the lawn outside the Punch and Judy booth which had been mistaken for a field latrine. This had been dispersed when the tent's single bulbous occupant still engaged in erecting it from the inside (the evident cause of the misunderstanding) had thrust his head through the proscenium opening and shouted at those in line—'Frig off, you!' Standing nearby, Treasure had debated again whether the man was entirely well cast as a children's entertainer.

Crabthorne, an early attendant, had advised that the other bus load of Sunfun Japanese would be along shortly, as soon—he had added bitterly—as they could be levered from their mass occupancy of the whirlpool. He had also volunteered that Patience had gone shopping in the High Street and would not be coming until later—an intelligence Treasure himself could have provided but with more accuracy.

Crutt, who had followed in Crabthorne's wake, had also come without his wife. He had waved timidly as though uncertain his greeting would be acknowledged, and when it was, mumbled apologetically that he believed Bronwen was with Patience—a possibility Treasure thought highly unlikely.

It was clear Crabthorne and Crutt considered their presence a matter of duty to the Judge: a misplaced assessment if ever there was one. The banker had left them as—without any apparent enthusiasm for the task or for each other's company—they had set off on a circuit of the garden.

It was at two minutes to three that Iffley appeared. He threaded his way through the mass of parked vehicles outside, then walked boldly over to Anna: he went through the motions of paying while conducting a rapid conversation with her. She several times shook her head, then motioned over her shoulder towards Treasure. Iffley stiffened momentarily. Next he followed Anna's glance. After his gaze met Treasure's he visibly relaxed and the characteristic half grin replaced a perplexed expression: it was Anna now who was doing all the talking.

The Inspector called a greeting and began to move towards Treasure. Simultaneously the banker picked up the throb of a motor-cycle close by and getting closer. The engine was being stifled then gunned alternately: it was an irritating noise.

There had been no one to notice that a few minutes earlier a man had entered the churchyard shed and that after a very short interval a woman had come out.

If anyone had been watching, it might have been observed the woman's attire was inappropriate for what had become a brilliantly sunny afternoon. She was dressed in a yellow, overall motor-cycling suit, black gauntlet gloves and mid-calf boots. Big dark glasses and a red silk scarf covered those parts of her face unmasked by a white crash helmet and pulled-down visor. Indeed, the only definitive clue to the sex of the individual inside all the cocooning was the name Barbara emblazoned in flamboyant, coarse red lettering on the front of the helmet and the back of the suit.

The unremarkable lightweight motor-cycle had been parked just in from the High Street near the church gate. The over-dressed rider bestrode the machine, kick-started it, then threaded it through the mass of cars parked with almost perverse irregularity along the narrow road to the New Hall gate.

'Windsor Castle,' said the rider, 'and pronto.'

Anna passed over the briefcase without hesitation as it was arranged she should. It was the same oddly high-pitched voice that had issued the instructions on the telephone.

Momentarily distracted by the approach of the Inspector, Treasure cursed himself for his fractionally slow reaction: so that was how it had been planned. 'Quick, man. Stop the motor-bike,' he snapped as he hurled himself past Iffley.

But already the machine was roaring away towards the farm track, and on a straight course with—remarkably—nothing parked to hinder it. Swiftly it disappeared around the rear end of the motor coach which had ultimately been backed to where it effectively closed the tapering road to everything else on four wheels.

Anna caught up with the two men who had raced past her to the end of the made-up road. She faced Iffley. 'Why didn't you run the other way when you had the chance, you bastard.' She slapped him hard across the face.

'Because, like I told you on the 'phone—' he dropped his voice—'I didn't know anything had happened to Ralph. D'you think I'd have come here? I'd have stopped that bike if I'd known—'

'Well here's your chance,' Treasure interrupted. 'It's coming back. This lane's blocked solid further down.'

The Vicar's car had done its job against even everything on two wheels.

It was the Inspector who made the bravest try. When the bike came up the lane at full throttle—the rider head down and determined—it swerved around Treasure who was standing ahead of the others. He grabbed at the pillion seat but failed to keep a grip.

Iffley was facing the machine after Treasure was out-manoeuvred and threw himself at the rider. Anna screamed as the bike swung round in a full circle with the policeman clutching at any handhold and 'Barbara' punching and kicking him while battling to keep the machine upright.

'Jump, Anna!' It was Treasure who shouted and who could see the bike's thrashing back wheel skidding ominously towards her. It was the warning that distracted Iffley for a fateful moment: he lost his hold—and very nearly some fingers—as the rider countered the skid, gunned the engine to bursting-point, and broke free, leaving the Inspector lying flat in the lane, his right hand bleeding profusely, his face badly cut and suffused with pain.

'Anna, look after him,' Treasure called as he started back up the lane, confident there was no quick way out now, even for a motor-cycle.

The rider raced on around the parked coach and then along the clear way as far as the New Hall gate. Treasure's prediction was even more accurate than he had imagined. A woman in charge of a wide pushchair bearing two-year-old twin girls bound for the Punch and Judy show was doing her best to angle the contraption through the only road space available.

The motor-cyclist swung into the drive of the big house accelerating across it and showering gravel in all directions: this was what woke Devalera. Next, without hesitation, the rider pointed the machine down the near, east

side of the house barely reducing speed as the bike swerved
between astonished visitors and crashed through the Lady
Setons, horn blaring and Devalera barking in counter-
point as he brought up the rear, unsure of the game but
happy to follow anything that went over flower-beds
unadmonished.

The terrace gained, under the incredulous gaze of the
Mesdames Evans and Ogmore-Davies (frozen, both of
them, in mid-pouring), the fugitive and following hound
then had a clear run down the three shallow stone steps
between the rose-beds to the lawn.

If the Punch and Judy man had pitched his booth on
the grass, as instructed, instead of on the dry gravel path
leading from the lawn to the lower shrub walks, the thing
would not have been snagged at one corner and upended
by the thrusting machine: but he hadn't, and it was. The
audience, half children and half Osakan, was delighted
by this turn in events. The Japanese, at least, assumed
that running over the tent was part of the traditional performance.

The puppeteer, buried under collapsed canvas and
flowering rhododendrons was first stupefied with rage but
then fortunately rendered speechless with fright. When
attempting to extricate himself from the tangle and while
still on his back he found himself staring into the eyes of a
gargantuan dog whose giant tongue was taste-testing his
chin. Devalera had abandoned the new game in favour of
cementing a predestined friendship with the largest
human being it had ever been his good fortune to fall
upon.

The Judge, who was standing nearby, being satisfied
that no one was injured, singularly resigned about the
passage of a careering, mad motor-cyclist through his
garden on visiting day and disappointed in the reduced
professional standard of the returned emigrant after a
year in Canada (or was it Australia?), turned firmly

towards the house. His mind was made up. He should
have had the dummy on hand for an emergency performance after all. He set off to fetch his new toy, audibly
repeating 'Another fine mess you've got us into, Stanley . . .'

Further down the garden, the unexpected eruption of
the fast moving motor-bike scattered the strollers on the
narrow paths ahead like so much chaff before an Arctic
wind.

Crutt and Crabthorne, taken completely unawares,
together jumped backwards to land ankle deep in a just
turned tump of rotted, wet compost: a not unsuitable fate
for purveyors of foot deodorant.

The lower garden gate, the motor-cyclist's evident objective, was set in the wall on the corner of the side road
and the High Street. There was a Boy Scout in charge of
it commissioned to direct outsiders to the main entrance
further along but also to unlock it for visitors wanting to
leave that way. On hearing—then seeing—the bike bearing down upon him he quickly prepared to meet its rider's
clear intention by throwing open the gate. The machine
shot by him at a dangerous speed.

The driver of the second coach-load of Japanese, a
Londoner, was on his first visit to the area. His instructions were to turn left at a church a mile east from the
Sunfun Hotel on the edge of Panty proper. He was not
exceeding any speed limit but he was late delivering his
charges. He had only once driven the road—in the opposite direction—and he had it in his mind that the turning he wanted was beyond and not before the church.

The German tourist coming the other way in the large
Mercedes was quite well aware he had to drive on the left
in Britain—and had been doing so since Dover. Even so,
he had been moving at a snail's pace in the solid line of
traffic going west for the last thirty minutes: in all that
time no single vehicle had passed him heading east. The
last part of Panty hill seemed to widen beyond the church

on the right just ahead. Although he couldn't quite see around the following bend he decided to risk it, pulled out, and accelerated.

If the coach driver had been slowing for the turn *before* the church, if the German car had not been moving so fast, if the road had really widened instead of narrowed at the bend, but if—above all—the yellow-clad motor-cyclist appearing from nowhere had not vacillated between a left or right direction with the machine on the crown of the High Street, an accident might have been avoided.

Treasure, still on foot, was only fifty yards from the scene. He had kept running between the parked cars. He had expected the fugitive to reappear from that gate. He saw the front of the coach hit the light machine, catapulting its rider sideways under the wheels of the Mercedes, an instant before the two big vehicles locked with a reverberating crunch of metal, and a sickening squeal of brakes.

The banker swallowed back the nausea. 'God help you, Lewin,' he whispered aloud: there was no one else to hear.

CHAPTER 21

'More tea, darling?' Molly Treasure refilled her husband's cup without waiting for a reply. Then she returned to studying the Cassatt sketch that had arrived carefully packaged at their breakfast table along with the letter from Henry Nott-Herbert that Treasure had just set aside.

It was Saturday, they were in their Chelsea home, and it was two weeks on from the weekend the banker had spent at Panty. Both plays in which Molly was performing at Chichester were out of the repertory for a few days: she had driven home late the night before. He had been in the USA for more than a week: they felt they had deserved each other's company—and a lingering breakfast.

Molly's consuming interest had been in the Panty episode even before Mrs Pink had brought in the mail.

'Your nice Judge must be immensely grateful to have sent you this.'

Treasure glanced again at the drawing. He had finished debating whether they could accept it: he had decided they should. 'He knows I fell in love with it—*and* it happens to have an absolutely impeccable provenance,' he added defensively, as though someone might have protested otherwise. 'By the way, Henry says he and Anna are getting married next month. Quietly.'

'And you think that's the right thing?'

'There's no cause or impediment . . .'

'You mean now her husband's gone for good,' Molly offered brightly—too brightly—before seeming to ponder for a moment. He had so far given her only a very incomplete outline of the story. They had few secrets from each other but he had pressed the need for a total and

permanent seal on this one. 'And you've given the money
back to her insurance company in New York. Wasn't that
tricky?'

He smiled. 'Even eminently respectable insurance companies will take money back without too much questioning. It's a fallacy to assume—'

'Especially from an even more respectable inter-
mediary?'

'Something like that, yes. It happens this particular
company—'

'Is the kind to take the money and run.' She spread
more butter than seemed necessary or desirable on a
small wedge of toast, considered it, covered it with mar-
malade, smiled at it forgivingly and transferred it to her
mouth in a delicate gesture. 'And Hutstacker's now own
Rigley and Whatsit?'

'Since last Thursday. Edgar Crabthorne nearly had a
fit when one of Henry's widowed cousins claimed at the
last minute she'd lost her share certificates—in a Zeppelin
raid in nineteen-sixteen. That really got the Telexes buzz-
ing. Actually the shares were in a bank.' He contemplated
the solitary boiled egg set before him. He still thought
back wistfully to Mrs Evans's breakfast extravaganzas.

'The Crabthornes left in a terrible hurry. Patience
telephoned from the airport on the Sunday morning.'
Molly eyed another piece of toast but decided to resist it.
There was luck in being 37 and still naturally slim and
lithe as well as unwrinkled, but one didn't push it too far.

'Their leaving reduced the numbers of people here who
could or would identify that body.'

'You said Patience—'

'Told me she was certain it was Spring after we came
from the hospital mortuary. But she told no one else
except her husband, and that was after Lewin's death.
That was why they went home next day. You don't ex-
tradite people to identify corpses.' He sipped his tea.

'Apparently Crutt only thought he'd seen Spring in the hotel corridor. Didn't remember who it might have been till later, and wasn't sure even then. He told Crabthorne though, who knew it must have been Spring—'

'Because he'd seen him outside the cathedral with you?'

'And chased after him. But Crutt wouldn't swear it was Spring he saw, and he certainly doesn't know the man he did see is dead.'

Molly looked puzzled. 'But he may still think Spring could be alive?'

Treasure nodded. 'Except he has a nice fat contract and pension scheme to remind him he's forgotten the whole incident—which, incidentally, he may have done anyway.'

'Did you . . . ?'

'No, I wasn't privy to that little deal but I'm certain that's what happened.' He grimaced. 'Earlier I'd had the idea there was something fishy about the time Crutt had taken to park his car that evening. I was quite wrong. That's exactly what he was doing.'

'And at the inquest the verdict was accidental death.'

'Mm. Despite the medical evidence, which could have suggested something different. It was death my misadventure on an unidentified body. Two taxi-drivers and three employees of the Sunfun Hotel recognized Spring as a visitor they'd served, but that was all. He was registered in the name of Brown.'

'And people don't go rushing round to morgues looking for loose relatives unless they've actually lost one,' Molly continued more casually. 'Anna Spring might—'

'Anna would have identified her husband if we hadn't known the murderer himself had died. There was no point.' He paused. 'I'm sure Inspector Iffley would have done the same. That is, ex-Detective-Inspector Iffley.'

' "And then there were none," ' quoted Molly. 'Except of course Constable Lewin. I still don't see how you were so certain he'd killed Spring. I mean, sending Patience to watch his house that afternoon, and getting the Vicar to block the lane.'

Treasure chuckled. 'Actually I thought he might be sending a woman on a push-bike to coast home down that farm track. There was no money in the case, of course, nor passport—that was destroyed.' He felt for his after-breakfast pipe before remembering again he didn't smoke. 'It was Spring who gave Lewin away by not wearing his disguise *after* the train business. He'd figured he was less likely to be recognized without disguise by people he needed to avoid or who meant him harm.'

'What about the Crabthornes and Crutt?'

'He had no idea they'd be in Panty and I don't believe he remembered Crutt. He thought Iffley and his hoodlums might be gunning for him, though. They'd be looking for a clergyman. Running into me might have complicated things too after what happened on the train. He'd been too dazed at the time to know I'd—how do they say?—penetrated his disguise. It wasn't me he ran from at the cathedral. It was the unexpected Crabthornes.'

'He wouldn't think Mrs Spring would be out to harm him?' Molly was as yet uncertain about Anna Spring in a number of contexts.

'His own wife? Certainly not,' Treasure replied with more vehemence than seemed quite necessary. 'So Lewin was the only one left—'

'Who'd seen him before without make-up, or whatever he was wearing.'

'Exactly, and it didn't bother him because he thought of Lewin as an ally—or at least a paid helper. Lewin knew who he was from the night of Ogmore-Davies's death. Next day he used his initiative . . .'

'Was he so much brighter than people thought?'

'Much. He got hold of Spring's London 'phone number . . .'

'How? Surely he's not in the book.'

'Lewin got the number the same way I did. By looking for it in Anna's address book. He'd have had plenty of opportunities the morning after the Captain's death while she was in the kitchen or the bedroom. It was listed beside the single letter R in the S section. The only London number in that section and one of the few in the book without a full name and address attached.'

'How amateur of Mrs Spring.'

'I figured that was the way you'd have done it.'

'Pig!' Molly pretended outrage, then added thoughtfully, 'I suppose I might have too.' She pulled a face. 'More poisoned tea?'

He nodded, smiling. 'It couldn't have taken long for Lewin to see the situation—that Iffley was cutting Spring out with his wife . . .'

'But there had to be insurance money . . .'

'Right. I think Lewin was playing both sides all through. Iffley was paying him but Spring was his big fish from the time he had 'phone contact. Since Iffley was getting Anna . . .'

'And Anna was getting the Judge,' Molly put in lightly, 'it followed that Spring would get most of the money. Did Lewin know the date of the fatal visit?'

'Probably not the actual date in advance. Spring doesn't seem to have trusted anyone that much.' He remembered the now evident fiction of the note to Scotland Yard. 'Like the others, Lewin probably knew Spring was due soon and that when he left it would be with his share of the money.'

'Perhaps Spring hoped he'd be able to come and go without Lewin knowing . . . without his having to pay him anything before disappearing for ever.'

'Quite possibly. But the episode on the train spoiled all that. After deciding to press on, I mean not to turn back, Spring felt he needed someone to protect him once he'd got the money. So he rang Lewin, I expect from the hotel, and arranged to have a real policeman pick him up after the pay-off in the cathedral. And that was his fatal error. He probably told Lewin exactly what was happening and offered him a percentage of the money. He could hardly appreciate the chap was planning to get the lot. To Lewin it must have looked like the perfect crime.'

'But there was no pay-off. You said . . .'

'Anna also rang Lewin in desperation. She told him to head off Spring if he could find him because of the Crab-thornes. She even left her car with the key in at the closest point so he could whisk her husband away.'

'But he didn't find him. I mean, Spring ran away of his own accord when he saw Edgar.'

'Right. Lewin made no effort to find him. He decided to take the chance Spring wouldn't be recognized by anyone. He stuck by his own original plan . . .'

'You mean to pick up Spring *after* he'd collected the money, drive him away and . . . and push him over a cliff.'

'Hit him over the head and then push him over a cliff into a cove—there are about a dozen perfect ones close by. He had the bonus too that he didn't need to do his dirty work in his Panda police car. Oh, and he made time to burgle Mrs Ogmore-Davies's—to lift the only picture of Spring that seemed to have survived, partly so he could destroy it, and partly so he could be sure of recognizing the chap . . .'

'Whom he'd only seen once. At night.'

'Yes. He had obviously unlatched that window himself from the inside when we were all leaving earlier.'

Molly took the piece of toast after all, broke it in two and put the smaller piece back in the silver rack. 'But Spring still arrived without the money.'

'Birth of Lewin's second plan—to dispose of Spring while he had the opportunity and pick up the money some other way. And he nearly worked it. Unaided.'

'You said Mrs Spring was certain a woman 'phoned.'

'She found Lewin's falsetto very convincing. I'd been told he sang counter-tenor and it stuck in my mind for some reason. Lewin and his wife didn't get on. I couldn't believe he'd have brought her in on a murder plan. He didn't. Apparently she'd left him for the third time a week before—the reason, incidentally, everybody's opted for his going berserk on a motor-bike. Emotional upset.'

'In fact, with his wife away he had a clear field.'

'And nearly put me off the scent at one point with that platinum watch he left on the body. It was what Iffley would have done, or Crutt, or almost anybody else who might have been involved.'

'To make it look like a bathing accident.'

'Exactly. I couldn't credit Lewin would chuck away a couple of thousand pounds' worth of watch until I remembered his saying he'd thought it was aluminium.'

Molly was nibbling at the toast without butter. 'Iffley was your second choice in villains?'

Treasure smiled. 'Not really. He's not even what's called a bent copper. I've made discreet enquiries about him at a very high level—'

'From Colin Bantree.' Molly's interruption was a mite deflating. Detective Chief Superintendent Bantree and his wife were old friends of both the Treasures.

He left the point unacknowledged. 'Anyway, he's highly thought of and his superiors are sorry he's leaving the Force. He's a bit unconventional. Even by current police standards. But he gets results.' He noted the emphasized lift of the eyebrows. 'And this isn't *Private Lives* and you don't have to play Amanda for your doting public again till Thursday.' The mock surprise turned into affected incomprehension. 'The chap's doing sterling work as a loner, but he's—'

'According to you he's been behaving exactly as he

pleases, having clergymen assaulted on trains . . .' Treasure had opened his mouth to protest. 'All right, bogus clergymen. He's been suborning his subordinates . . . er . . . even before they turn into murderers.' She paused, conscious of a weak case. 'Ah. He's been frightening old ladies, seducing young ones, and doing a nice line in fine art on the company's time — not to mention complicity in insurance fraud, lurking around cathedrals — you said — when he was supposed to be somewhere else, and . . . and . . .'

'His car was parked where I saw it at what they call The Popples because it had broken down there earlier. He'd been in St David's trying to find out where Spring was staying and left the car after whistling up a spare from the local police pool. He wasn't trying to double-cross anybody.' He paused. 'Of course what you say is relatively true, but it's about the most uncharitable interpretation one could apply.'

'And you're ready to forgive and forget?'

Treasure nodded. 'Partly for the way he tackled Lewin and the motor-bike. That took some courage. To be honest, when he turned up at New Hall I thought he and Lewin might be in league. I didn't know he'd talked to Anna on the 'phone just before. She'd already practically accused him of murder. Anyway, he's paying for his indiscretions by resigning his job. He's lost Anna — really lost her. For her he was a passing infatuation.' He caught Molly's sceptical expression. 'Emotionally she's pretty unstable.' The expression changed to one of pretended pity. 'Incidentally,' he was returning to firmer ground, 'the resignation was my idea. Iffley expected I'd turn him in. I said that wouldn't help anybody but I really thought he'd be happier in a different line of work.'

'Like buying and selling pictures?'

'Yes, as a matter of fact. He has the flair for it and the nose.' He shrugged his shoulders. 'You see, nobody would have gained if everything had had to come out. Even Mrs

Ogmore-Davies would have suffered by losing an illusion or two. I didn't tell you, her arch enemy Mrs Pugh says the Captain was trying to borrow carpet tacks from her husband, the landlord of the Boatman, the night he died. He'd decided to do away with the rods they had on the stairs at Mariner's Rest, but he'd run out of tacks.' He chuckled. 'So it wasn't a spirit that moved the stair-rods to the kitchen table. It was the poor old Captain when his wife was out.'

He picked up the Judge's letter, then looked seriously at Molly. 'You're going to say I've been playing God in all this.'

'Again.' She smiled and shrugged her shoulders. 'I should hate to have to play Anna Spring in the film of the book. An enigmatic character.' They both knew that so long as British audiences continued flocking to watch their favourite interpreter of upper-crust comedy—from Congreve to Douglas Home—the need for Molly to test her art in high drama was happily remote. 'Did she just charm you into arranging the cosy ending or did she offer more torrid inducements?' Torrid was one of Molly's favourite words. She lit a cigarette.

'Smoking can damage your health . . .'

'Not on Saturdays. So obviously she offered more torrid inducements.'

'Nonsense. There were moments . . .'

'Darling, I trust you. Remember? I'm sure it was good for your ego whatever happened. I'm not so confident about the poor little Judge. Let's face it, there's a lot he doesn't know about his future wife.'

Treasure ruffled through the pages of Nott-Herbert's letter. 'I'm not sure. Anna intends to tell him every-thing—in her own time. Well, almost everything.'

'Or so she says.'

'Or unless he stops her. Listen to this.' He scanned one of the pages for the passage he was seeking. 'He writes:

"When a beautiful young woman consents to marry a comparatively rich and decidedly old man, and then refuses to name a date, there has to be a reason. Whatever Anna's reason was it has now disappeared, I choose to believe, thanks to your visit.

' "This is exactly as Bishop Clarence Wringle anticipated. You will know, by the by, that the business of Mrs Ogmore-Davies was a harmless camouflage. The lady was of course mistaken over what she saw that morning in March. Even so, I sensed that what is best described as Anna's disquiet was in some measure to do with the Ogmore-Davies *oeuvre*, and that it would be appropriate to have you crack that particular shell." '

Treasure looked up. 'Now mark this next passage. "I have no illusions about the apparently inappropriate matching of Anna and myself. Although it will give me enormous pride to honour her as my wife for that part of life which remains to me, I have gone to some trouble to enquire into the use of discretionary trusts, and being satisfied that financially Anna could be nearly as well provided for in this way without marrying me—thus being free to marry someone else without great penalty—I have offered her the option. She will have none of it.

' "Clearly I am not displeased. Anna is perhaps in need of what is termed a father figure after what has been in recent years a trying episode. I can certainly fill that role just as Anna can fill a similar one in the matter of the boy Aneurin—or Nye as we call him. They are inordinately fond of each other.

' "Anna, as you know, is childless and for delicate physiological reasons, which need not detain us, will sadly remain so. You may know also I lost my only son who died with his wife in an accident some years ago. The marriage was without issue but it has always been my belief that Nye was the result of a liaison between my son, before his marriage, and the boy's mother. The woman, Mrs Evans's daughter, has always refused to confirm this, but to me she has not denied it either.

' "By the by, the suggestion which may have reached you, that Nye resembles the late Captain Ogmore-Davies is perfectly tenable. Ogmore-Davies was some sort of cousin to Mrs Evans.

' "In any event, with the consent of the mother and the enthusiastic approval of Anna and the boy, not to mention the grandmother and Mrs Ogmore-Davies, we propose formally to adopt Nye after Anna and I are married." '

Treasure looked up. 'He then goes on about the picture. Hopes you like it too and that we'll visit them soon. Oh, and he's taking a correspondence course in photography.'

Molly smiled. 'I think Mrs Spring may find she's marrying a man who's discovering the secret of enduring life.'

'You mean so long as one's ready to start on new things? Did I tell you he has a whole chapel organ in the hall he hasn't a notion how to drive!' He chuckled. 'He's acquired a new camera. Encloses a picture of Anna. It hardly does her justice.' He passed the coloured print to his wife while regretting the last comment.

Molly studied it for a moment. The eyebrows had arched again. 'What a very c—'

'Common. You're going to say she's common. I knew it.'

Molly looked across the table in innocent surprise. 'Darling, I was going to say what a classic beauty. The high cheek-bones. Those big soulful eyes. I can't imagine why you should think her common.'

'I was only—' Treasure had scarcely begun his protest when Molly interrupted.

'Pity West Wales is so inaccessible. Patience said the places were lovely but the travelling purgatory.' She glanced down again at Anna's picture. 'We must thank

them for the drawing but let's not commit about a visit . . .
not for some time.' Then after favouring her husband
with one of the most famous, practised and disarming of
smiles she added earnestly, 'I do hope they'll be very, very
happy.'

F   Williams, David
Wil
        Murder for treasure

                            75,986